Horace McCoy was born near Nashville, Tennessee in 1897. During his lifetime he travelled all over the US as a salesman and taxi-driver, and his varied career included reporting and sports editing, acting as bodyguard to a politician, doubling for a wrestler, and writing for films and magazines. His novels include *I Should Have Stayed Home* (1938), *Kiss Tomorrow Goodbye* (1948), and *They Shoot Horses, Don't They?* (1935), which was made into a film. He died in 1955.

T0118279

Praise for Horace McCoy

'Aficionados of hard-boiled fiction who think that Hammett, Cain, and Jim Thompson set the standard ought to take a look at Horace McCoy' *Kirkus*

'Horace McCoy shoots words like bullets' *Time*

'A spare, bleak parable about American life, which McCoy pictured as a Los Angeles dance marathon in the early thirties . . . full of the kind of apocalyptic detail that both he and Nathanael West saw in life as lived on the Hollywood fringe' *New York Times*

'Captures the survivalist barbarity in this bizarre convention, and becomes a metaphor for life itself: the last couple on their feet gets the prize' *Independent*

'I was moved, then shaken by the beauty and genius of Horace McCoy's metaphor' *Village Voice*

'It's the unanswerable nature of the whydunnit that ensures the book's durability' *Booklit.com*

'Takes the reader into one of America's darkest corners . . . The story has resonance for contemporary America and the current craze for reality television. How far are we from staging a dance marathon for television?' *readywhenyouarecb.com*

'This almost sadistically frank pulp fiction from 1935 will cure anyone of the delusion that earlier generations didn't know the score. With murder, incest, abortion, and the like generously added to a plot about people entertaining themselves by watching the misery of others, it's like one of these eliminationist "reality" television shows (*Survivor*, *Big Brother*, etc.) as conceived by the creative team of Thomas Hobbes and Charles Darwin. These lives are indeed nasty, brutish, and short. It doesn't make for a pretty story, but you have to admire the zeal and energy with which Horace McCoy drives his point home' *Brothersjudd.com*

They Shoot HORSES Don't They?

HORACE McCOY

Introduction by John Harvey

First published in the USA in 1935
First published in the UK in 1938

First published in 1995 by Serpent's Tail
First published in this edition in 2010 by Serpent's Tail,
an imprint of Profile Books Ltd
3A Exmouth House
Pine Street
London EC1R 0JH
website: www.serpentstail.com

ISBN 978 1 84668 739 6

introduction

I first became aware of Horace McCoy, appropriately enough, through the movies: as the writer upon whose novel the violent and unforgiving 1950 film *Kiss Tomorrow Goodbye* was based, and as one of the two principal scriptwriters on *The Lusty Men*, which shows director Nicholas Ray and actor Robert Mitchum at their absolute best. Appropriately, for McCoy was in many ways a movie man, initially as a struggling extra and bit-part player and later, more successfully, as a screenwriter. It was this close-quarters experience of the Hollywood studios, of course, that furnished him with the material for his first, and still best-known novel, *They Shoot Horses, Don't They?* (1935) and the later, not wholly dissimilar, *I Should Have Stayed Home* (1938).

I bought my first copy of *They Shoot Horses, Don't They?* in the mid-sixties, at a time when I was snapping up as many of the Penguin green jacket crime series as I could – those by American authors, in particular. I had read my way through Hammett and Chandler and was looking for anything similarly racy and hard-boiled, and the cover, with its smiling, hopeful female face partly obliterated by the blood-red centre of a target, suggested that here I would find what I was looking for.

So I did, and more besides.

For one thing, the smiling face was completely, utterly wrong. Gloria Beatty may once have smiled, once have harboured optimistic thoughts about her future, but not here. From her first fateful meeting with Robert, the story's narrator – 'Let's go sit and hate a bunch of people' – through to her climactic rage against the women from the Mothers' League for Good Morals, Gloria drives the story with a tremendous negative energy that wells up from her understanding that the world – her world, the world that plays out beneath the Hollywood sign – is one of amorality and illusion.

Even before arriving at my understanding of Gloria's almost complete nihilism (and how brilliant of McCoy that he can keep us interested for so long in a character who cares about little or nothing, including herself), I think I realised that what I had in my hand was a book that was in some ways extraordinary. This is signalled clearly from the beginning – the first words from the courtroom presented starkly on their own page, followed immediately by the narrator's remembrance of Gloria's murder, and then the judge's words which will lead inexorably towards the final sentence (growing larger and bolder on the page as they do so, thanks to the original book's designer, Philip Van Doren Stern), these alternating with passages which move between the events leading up to the shooting, reminiscences of Robert's past, and descriptions of what is going on in the courtroom.

Again, McCoy's technique is superb here, never deviating from the tightness of focus and expression he would have learned in his early days labouring (along with

Chandler, Hammett and others) at *Black Mask* magazine under its editor, Joseph T. Shaw, yet moving us effortlessly, nevertheless, between time and place, between long shot and close-up.

It's little wonder that McCoy was taken up with particular seriousness in France, where he was raised to the same pantheon as Faulkner and Hemingway, the mixture of fatalism and realism in his work seen as the burgeoning of American existentialism. In the United States, he was far more likely to be linked with another writer of noirish tales from the years of the Depression, James M. Cain, a comparison with which McCoy was less than happy. As he informed his publishers, if they continued to label him as being 'of the Cain school', he would be forced either to slit Cain's throat or his own.

What McCoy's work exhibits, more clearly perhaps than that of Cain or any other of the hard-boiled American writers, with the possible exception of Hammett, is a strong and clearly expressed sense of the ways in which the fate of individuals is inextricably linked to broader political and social movements, a strongly left-wing, anti-capitalist stance being most clearly expressed in *No Pockets in a Shroud*, based upon his time as a newspaper man, in which the journalist hero is murdered to prevent him from exposing the truth. There is also a lightness of touch within the harshness of the world McCoy depicts. As he stated in an address to aspiring writers, reported in the *Pasadena Star-News*, one of his prime intentions when writing was 'dwelling on the lyrical quality that lies in any dramatic action and the transfer of that lyrical quality to the pages of a book by means of graphic and telling words'.

What all of this means is that you have in your hands a remarkable novel, worthy of admiration, both as an example of the writer's craft and as a portrait of a particular time and milieu.

With *They Shoot Horses, Don't They?* and, perhaps to a lesser extent, *I Should Have Stayed Home*, McCoy has made a place for himself alongside other writers of the period, such as Nathanael West, John O'Hara or F. Scott Fitzgerald, who sought to shine a light through the miasma of Hollywood and, through that, the perils and falsities of the American Dream.

They Shoot
Horses
Don't They?

The prisoner will stand . . .

...*chapter one*

I stood up. For a moment I saw Gloria again, sitting on that bench on the pier. The bullet had just struck her in the side of the head; the blood had not even started to flow. The flash from the pistol still lighted her face. Everything was as plain as day. She was completely relaxed, was completely comfortable. The impact of the bullet had turned her head a little away from me; I did not have a perfect profile view but I could see enough of her face and her lips to know she was smiling. The Prosecuting Attorney was wrong when he told the jury she died in agony, friendless, alone except for her brutal murderer, out there in that black night on the edge of the Pacific. He was as wrong as a man can be. She did not die in agony. She was relaxed and comfortable and she was smiling. It was the first time I had ever seen her smile. How could she have been in agony then? And she wasn't friendless.

I was her very best friend. I was her only friend. So how could she have been friendless?

. . . is there any legal cause why
sentence should not now be pronounced?

...*chapter two*

What could I say? . . . All those people knew I had killed her; the only other person who could have helped me at all was dead too. So I just stood there, looking at the judge and shaking my head. I didn't have a leg to stand on.

'Ask the mercy of the court,' said Epstein, the lawyer they had assigned to defend me.

'What was that?' the judge said.

'Your Honour,' Epstein said, ' – we throw ourselves on the mercy of the court. This boy admits killing the girl, but he was only doing her a personal favour – '

The judge banged on the desk, looking at me.

There being no legal cause why sentence should not now be pronounced . . .

...*chapter three*

It was funny the way I met Gloria. She was trying to get into pictures too, but I didn't know that until later. I was walking down Melrose one day from the Paramount studios when I heard somebody hollering, 'Hey! Hey!' and I turned around and there she was running towards me and waving. I stopped, waving back. When she got up to me she was all out of breath and excited and I saw I didn't know her.

'Damn that bus,' she said.

I looked around and there was the bus half a block down the street going towards Western.

'Oh,' I said, 'I thought you were waving at me . . .'

'What would I be waving at you for?' she asked.

I laughed. 'I don't know,' I said. 'You going my way?'

'I may as well walk on down to Western,' she said; and we began to walk on down towards Western.

That was how it all started and it seems very strange to me now. I don't understand it at all. I've thought and thought and still I don't understand it. This wasn't murder. I try to do somebody a favour and I wind up getting myself killed. *They are going to kill me. I know exactly what the judge is going to say. I can tell by the look of him that he is*

7

*going to be glad to say it and I can tell by the feel of the
people behind me that they are going to be glad to hear him
say it.*

Take that morning I met Gloria. I wasn't feeling very
good; I was still a little sick, but I went over to Paramount
because von Sternberg was making a Russian picture and I
thought maybe I could get a job. I used to ask myself what
could be nicer than working for von Sternberg, or Mamoulian or Boleslawsky either, getting paid to watch him direct,
learning about composition and tempo and angles . . . so I
went over to Paramount.

I couldn't get inside, so I hung around the front until noon
when one of his assistants came out for lunch. I caught up with
him and asked what was the chance to get some atmosphere.

'None,' he said, telling me that von Sternberg was very
careful about his atmospheric people.

I thought that was a lousy thing to say but I knew what he
was thinking, that my clothes didn't look any too good.
'Isn't this a costume picture?' I asked.

'All our extras come through Central,' he said, leaving
me . . .

I wasn't going anywhere in particular; I was just riding
along in my Rolls-Royce, having people point me out as the
greatest director in the world, when I heard Gloria hollering.
You see how those things happen?

So we walked on down Melrose to Western, getting
acquainted all the time; and when we got to Western I knew
she was Gloria Beatty, an extra who wasn't doing well either,
and she knew a little about me. I liked her very much.

She had a small room with some people over near Beverly and I lived only a few blocks from there, so I saw her again that night. That first night was really what did it but even now I can't honestly say I regret going to see her. I had about seven dollars I had made squirting soda in a drug store (subbing for a friend of mine. He had got a girl in a jam and had to take her to Santa Barbara for the operation.) and I asked her if she'd rather go to a movie or sit in the park.

'What park?' she asked.

'It's right over here a little way,' I said.

'All right,' she said. 'I got a bellyful of moving pictures anyway. If I'm not a better actress than most of those dames I'll eat your hat – Let's go sit and hate a bunch of people . . .'

I was glad she wanted to go to the park. It was always nice there. It was a fine place to sit. It was very small, only one block square, but it was very dark and very quiet and filled with dense shrubbery. All around it palm trees grew up, fifty, sixty feet tall, suddenly tufted at the top. Once you entered the park you had the illusion of security. I often imagined they were sentries wearing grotesque helmets: my own private sentries, standing guard over my own private island . . .

The park was a fine place to sit. Through the palms you could see many buildings, the thick, square silhouettes of apartment houses, with their red signs on the roofs, reddening the sky above and everything and everybody below. But if you wanted to get rid of these things you had only to sit and stare at them with a fixed gaze . . . and they would begin receding. That way you could drive them as far into the distance as you wanted to . . .

'I never paid much attention to this place before,' Gloria said.

. . . 'I like it,' I said, taking off my coat and spreading it on the grass for her. 'I come here three or four times a week.'

'You do like it,' she said, sitting down.

'How long you been in Hollywood?' I asked.

'About a year. I been in four pictures already. I'd have been in more,' she said, 'but I can't get registered by Central.'

'Neither can I,' I said.

Unless you were registered by Central Castings Bureau you didn't have much chance. The big studios call up Central and say they want four Swedes or six Greeks or two Bohemian peasant types or six Grand Duchesses and Central takes care of it. I could see why Gloria didn't get registered by Central. She was too blonde and too small and looked too old. With a nice wardrobe she might have looked attractive, but even then I wouldn't have called her pretty.

'Have you met anybody who can help you?' I asked.

'In this business how can you tell who'll help you?' she said. 'One day you're an electrician and the next day you're a producer. The only way I could ever get to a big shot would be to jump on the running board of his car as it passed by. Anyway, I don't know whether the men stars can help me as much as the women stars. From what I've seen lately I've about made up my mind that I've been letting the wrong sex try to make me. . . .'

'How'd you happen to come to Hollywood?' I asked.

'Oh, I don't know,' she said in a moment – 'but anything is an improvement over the life I led back home.' I asked her where that was. 'Texas,' she said. 'West Texas. Ever been there?'

'No,' I said, 'I come from Arkansas.'

'Well, West Texas is a hell of a place,' she said. 'I lived with my aunt and uncle. He was a brakeman on a railroad. I only saw him once or twice a week, thank God. . . .'

She stopped, not saying anything, looking at the red, vapourish glow above the apartment buildings.

'At least,' I said, 'you had a home – '

'That's what you call it,' she said. 'Me, I got another name for it. When my uncle was home he was always making passes at me and when he was on the road my aunt and I were always fighting. She was afraid I'd tattle on her – '

'Nice people,' I said to myself.

'So I finally ran away,' she said, 'to Dallas. Ever been there?'

'I've never been in Texas at all,' I said.

'You haven't missed anything,' she said. 'I couldn't get a job, so I decided to steal something in a store and make the cops take care of me.'

'That was a good idea,' I said.

'It was a swell idea,' she said, 'only it didn't work. I got arrested all right but the detectives felt sorry for me and turned me loose. To keep from starving to death I moved in with a Syrian who had a hot-dog place around the corner from the City Hall. He chewed tobacco all the time. . . . Have you ever been in bed with a man who chewed tobacco?'

'I don't believe I have,' I said.

'I guess I might even have stood that,' she said, 'but when he wanted to make me between customers, on the kitchen table, I gave up. A couple of nights later I took poison.'

'Jesus,' I said to myself.

'I didn't take enough,' she said. 'I only got sick. Ugh, I can still taste the stuff. I stayed in the hospital a week. That was where I got the idea of coming to Hollywood.'

'It was?' I said.

'From the movie magazines,' she said. 'After I got discharged I started hitch-hiking. Is that a laugh or not? . . .'

'That's a good laugh,' I said, trying to laugh. . .

'Haven't you got any parents?'

'Not any more,' she said. 'My old man got killed in the war in France. I wish I could get killed in a war.'

'Why don't you quit the movies?' I asked.

'Why should I?' she said. 'I may get to be a star overnight. Look at Hepburn and Margaret Sullavan and Josephine Hutchinson . . . but I'll tell you what I would do if I had the guts: I'd walk out of a window or throw myself in front of a street car or something.'

'I know how you feel,' I said; 'I know exactly how you feel.'

'It's peculiar to me,' she said, 'that everybody pays so much attention to living and so little to dying. Why are these high-powered scientists always screwing around trying to prolong life instead of finding pleasant ways to end it? There must be a hell of a lot of people in the world like me – who want to die but haven't got the guts – '

'I know what you mean,' I said; 'I know exactly what you mean.'

Neither of us said anything for a couple of seconds.

'A girl friend of mine has been trying to get me to enter a marathon dance down at the beach,' she said. 'Free food and free bed as long as you last and a thousand dollars if you win.'

'The free food part of it sounds good,' I said.

'That's not the big thing,' she said. 'A lot of producers and directors go to those marathon dances. There's always the chance they might pick you out and give you a part in a picture. . . What do you say?'

'Me?' I said . . . 'Oh, I don't dance very well. . . .'

'You don't have to. All you have to do is keep moving.'

'I don't think I better try it,' I said. 'I been pretty sick. I just got over the intestinal flu. I almost died. I was so weak I used to have to crawl to the john on my hands and knees. I don't think I better try it,' I said, shaking my head.

'When was all this?'

'A week ago,' I said.

'You're all right now,' she said.

'I don't think so – I better not try it, I'm liable to have a relapse.'

'I'll take care of that,' she said.

'. . . Maybe in a week – ' I said.

'It'll be too late then. You're strong enough now,' she said. . . .

. . . it is the judgment and sentence
of this court . . .

...*chapter four*

The marathon dance was held on the amusement pier at the beach in an enormous old building that once had been a public dance hall. It was built out over the ocean on pilings, and beneath our feet, beneath the floor, the ocean pounded night and day. I could feel it surging through the balls of my feet, as if they had been stethoscopes.

Inside was a dance space for the contestants, thirty feet wide and two hundred feet long, and around this on three sides were loge seats, behind these were the circus seats, the general admission. At the end of the dance space was a raised platform for the orchestra. It played only at night and was not a very good orchestra. During the day we had what music we could pick up with the radio, made loud by amplifiers. Most of the time it was too loud, filling the hall with noise. We had a master of ceremonies, whose duty it was to make the customers feel at home; two floor judges who moved around the floor all the time with the contestants to see that everything went all right, two male and female nurses, and a house doctor for emergencies. The doctor didn't look like a doctor at all. He was much too young.

One hundred and forty-four couples entered the marathon

dance but sixty-one dropped out for the first week. The rules were you danced for an hour and fifty minutes, then you had a ten-minute rest period in which you could sleep if you wanted to. But in those ten minutes you also had to shave or bathe or get your feet fixed or whatever was necessary.

The first week was the hardest. Everybody's feet and legs swelled and down beneath the ocean kept pounding, pounding against the pilings all the time. Before I went into this marathon dance I used to love the Pacific Ocean: its name, its size, its colour, its smell – I used to sit for hours looking at it, wondering about the ships that had sailed it and never returned, about China and the South Seas, wondering all sorts of things. . . . But not any more. I've had enough of the Pacific. I don't care whether I ever see it again or not. *I probably won't. The judge is going to take care of that.*

Gloria and I had been tipped off by some old-timers that the way to beat a marathon dance was to perfect a system for those ten-minute rest periods: learning to eat your sandwich while you shaved, learning to eat when you went to the john, when you had your feet fixed, learning to read newspapers while you danced, learning to sleep on your partner's shoulder while you were dancing; but these were all tricks of the trade you had to practise. They were very difficult for Gloria and me at first.

I found out that about half of the people in this contest were professionals. They made a business of going in marathon dances all over the country, some of them even hitch-hiking from town to town. The others were just girls and boys who came in like Gloria and me.

Couple No. 13 were our best friends in the dance. This was James and Ruby Bates, from some little town in northern Pennsylvania. It was their eighth marathon dance; they had won a $1,500 prize in Oklahoma, going 1,253 hours in continuous motion. There were several other teams in this dance who claimed championships of some kind, but I knew James and Ruby would be right in there for the finish. That is, if Ruby's baby didn't come first. She expected a baby in four months.

'What's the matter with Gloria?' James asked me one day as we came back to the floor from the sleeping quarters.

'Nothing. What do you mean?' I asked. But I knew what he meant. Gloria had been singing the blues again.

'She keeps telling Ruby what a chump she would be to have the baby,' he said. 'Gloria wants her to have an abortion.'

'I can't understand Gloria talking like that,' I said, trying to smooth things over.

'You tell her to lay off Ruby,' he said.

When the whistle started us off on the 216th hour I told Gloria what James had said.

'Nuts to him,' she said. 'What does he know about it?'

'I don't see why they can't have a baby if they want to. It's their business,' I said. 'I don't want to make James sore. He's been through a lot of these dances and he's already given us some good tips. Where would we be if he got sore?'

'It's a shame for that girl to have a baby,' Gloria said.

'What's the sense of having a baby unless you got dough enough to take care of it?'

'How do you know they haven't?' I asked.

'If they have what're they doing here? . . . That's the trouble now,' she said. 'Everybody is having babies – '

'Oh, not everybody,' I said.

'A hell of a lot you know about it. You'd been better off if you'd never been born – '

'Maybe not,' I said. 'How do you feel?' I asked, trying to get her mind off her troubles.

'I always feel lousy,' she said. 'God, the hand on the clock moves slow.' There was a big strip of canvas on the master of ceremonies' platform, painted in the shape of a clock, up to 2,500 hours. The hand now pointed to 216. Above it was a sign: ELAPSED HOURS – 216. COUPLES REMAINING – 83.

'How are your legs?'

'Still pretty weak,' I said. 'That flu is awful stuff.'

'Some of the girls think it'll take 2,000 hours to win,' Gloria said.

'I hope not,' I said. 'I don't believe I can hold out that long.'

'My shoes are wearing out,' Gloria said. 'If we don't hurry up and get a sponsor I'll be barefooted.' A sponsor was a company or a firm that gave you sweaters and advertised their names or products on the backs. Then they took care of your necessities.

James and Ruby danced over beside us. 'Did you tell her?' he asked, looking at me. I nodded.

'Wait a minute,' Gloria said, as they started to dance away. 'What's the big idea of talking behind my back?'

'Tell that twist to lay off me,' James said, still speaking directly to me.

Gloria started to say something else but before she could get it out I danced her away from there. I didn't want any scenes.

'The son of a bitch,' she said.

'He's sore,' I said. 'Now where are we?'

'Come on,' she said, 'I'll tell him where he gets off – '

'Gloria,' I said, 'will you please mind your own business?'

'Soft pedal that loud cussing,' a voice said. I looked around. It was Rollo Peters, the floor judge.

'Nuts to you,' Gloria said. Through my fingers I could feel the muscles twitching in her back, just like I could feel the ocean surging through the balls of my feet.

'Pipe down,' Rollo said. 'The people in the box can hear you. What do you think this is – a joint?'

'Joint is right,' Gloria said.

'All right, all right,' I said.

'I told you once already about the cussing,' Rollo said. 'I better not have to tell you again. It sounds bad to the customers.'

'Customers? Where are they?' Gloria said.

'You let us worry about that,' Rollo said, glaring at me.

'All right, all right,' I said.

He blew his whistle, stopping everybody from moving. Some of them were barely moving, just enough to keep from being disqualified. 'All right, kids,' he said, 'a little sprint.'

'A little sprint, kids,' the master of ceremonies, Rocky Gravo, said into the microphone. The noise of his voice in the amplifiers filled the hall, shutting out the pounding of the ocean. 'A little sprint – around the track you go – Give,' he said to the orchestra, and the orchestra began playing. The contestants started dancing with a little more animation.

The sprint lasted about two minutes and when it was finished Rocky led the applause, and then said into the microphone:

'Look at these kids, ladies and gentlemen – after 216 hours they are as fresh as a daisy in the world's championship marathon dance – a contest of endurance and skill. These kids are fed seven times a day – three big meals and four light lunches. Some of them have even gained weight while in the contest – and we have doctors and nurses constantly in attendance to see that they are in the best of physical condition. Now I'm going to call on Couple No. 4, Mario Petrone and Jackie Miller, for a specialty. Come on, Couple No. 4 – there they are, ladies and gentlemen. Isn't that a cute pair? . . .'

Mario Petrone, a husky Italian, and Jackie Miller, a little blonde, went up to the platform to some applause. They spoke to Rocky and then began a tap dance that was very bad. Neither Mario nor Jackie seemed conscious that it was bad. When it was over a few people pitched money onto the floor.

'Give, people,' Rocky said. 'A silver shower. Give.'

A few more coins hit the floor. Mario and Jackie picked them up, moving over near us.

'How much?' Gloria asked them.

'Feels like about six-bits,' Jackie said.

'Where you from, kid?' Gloria asked.

'Alabama.'

'I thought so,' Gloria said.

'You and I ought to learn a specialty,' I said to Gloria. 'We could make some extra money.'

'You're better off without knowing any,' Mario said. 'It only means extra work and it don't do your legs any good.'

'Did you all hear about the derbies?' Jackie asked.

'What are they?' I asked.

'Some kind of a race,' she said. 'I think they're going to explain them at the next rest period.'

'The cheese is beginning to bind,' Gloria said.

. . . that for the crime of murder in the first degree

...chapter
five

In the dressing room Rocky Gravo introduced Vincent (Socks) Donald, one of the promoters.

'Lissen, kids,' Socks said, 'don't none of you be discouraged because people ain't coming to the marathon dance. It takes time to get these things going, so we have decided to start a little novelty guaranteed to pack 'em in. Now here's what we're gonna do. We're gonna have a derby race every night. We're going to paint an oval on the floor and every night everybody will race around the track for fifteen minutes and the last couple every night is disqualified. I guarantee that'll bring in the crowds.'

'It'll bring in the undertaker, too,' somebody said.

'We'll move some cots out in the middle of the track,' the promoter said, 'and have the doctor and nurses on hand during the derby. When a contestant falls out and has to go to the pit, the partner will have to make two laps to make up for it. You kids will get more kick out of it because the crowds will be bigger. Say, when that Hollywood bunch starts coming here, we'll be standing 'em up. . . . Now, how's the food? Anybody got any kicks about anything? All right, kids, that's fine. You play ball with us and we'll play ball with you.'

We went out to the floor. None of the contestants had anything to say about the derbies. They seemed to think that anything was a good idea if it would only start the crowds to coming. Rollo came up to me as I sat down on the railing. I had about two minutes more of rest before the next two-hour grind.

'Don't get me wrong about what I said a few minutes ago,' he said. 'It's not you, it's Gloria.'

'I know,' I said. 'She's all right. She's just sore on the world, that's all.'

'Try to keep her piped down,' he said.

'That's a hard job, but I'll do the best I can,' I said.

In a moment I looked up to the runway from the girls' dressing room and I was surprised to see Gloria and Ruby coming to the floor together. I went over to meet her.

'What do you think about the derbies?' I asked her.

'It's one good way to kill us off,' she said.

The whistle started us away again.

'There's not more than a hundred people here tonight,' I said. Gloria and I weren't dancing. I had my arm around her shoulder and she had hers around my waist, walking. That was all right. For the first week we had to dance, but after that you didn't. All you had to do was keep moving. I saw James and Ruby coming over to us and I could tell by the expression on his face that something was wrong. I wanted to get away, but there was no place to go.

'I told you to lay off my wife, didn't I?' he said to Gloria.

'You go to hell, you big ape,' Gloria said.

'Wait a minute,' I said. 'What's the matter?'

'She's been after Ruby again,' James said. 'Every time I turn my back she's after her again.'

'Forget it, Jim,' Ruby said, trying to steer him away.

'Naw, I won't forget it. I told you to keep your mouth shut, didn't I?' he said to Gloria.

'You take a flying – '

Before Gloria could get the words finished he slapped her hard on the side of the face, knocking her head against my shoulder It was a hard wallop. I couldn't stand for that. I reached up and hit him in the mouth. He hit me in the jaw with his left hand, knocking me back against some of the dancers. That kept me from falling to the floor. He rushed at me and I grabbed him, wrestling with him, trying to jerk my knee up between his legs to foul him. It was the only chance I had.

A whistle blew in my ear and somebody grabbed us. It was Rollo Peters. He shoved us apart.

'Cut it out,' he said. 'What's coming off here?'

'Nothing,' I said.

'Nothing,' Ruby said.

Rollo raised his hand, waving to Rocky on the platform.

'Give,' said Rocky, and the orchestra started to play.

'Scatter out,' Rollo said to the contestants, who started to move away. 'Come on,' he said, leading them around the floor.

'Next time I'm going to cut your throat,' James said to Gloria.

'—you,' Gloria said.

25

'Shut up,' I said.

I walked away with her, down into a corner, where we slowed up, barely moving along.

'Are you crazy?' I said. 'Why don't you let Ruby alone?'

'Don't worry, I'm through wasting my breath on her. If she wants to have a deformed baby, that's okay by me.'

'Hello, Gloria,' a voice said.

We looked around. It was an old woman in a front row box seat by the railing. I didn't know her name but she was quite a character. She had been there every night, bringing her blanket and her lunch. One night she wrapped up in her blanket and stayed all night. She was about sixty-five years old.

'Hello,' Gloria said.

'What was the matter down there?' the old woman asked.

'Nothing,' Gloria said. 'Just a little argument.'

'How do you feel?' the old woman asked.

'All right, I guess,' Gloria replied.

'I'm Mrs Layden,' the old woman said. 'You're my favourite couple.'

'Well, thanks,' I said.

'I tried to enter this,' Mrs Layden said, 'but they wouldn't let me. They said I was too old, but I'm only sixty.'

'Well, that's fine,' I said.

Gloria and I had stopped, our arms around each other, swaying our bodies. You had to keep moving all the time. A couple of men moved into the loge behind the old woman. Both of them were chewing unlighted cigars.

'They're dicks,' Gloria said under her breath.

'. . . How do you like the contest?' I asked Mrs Layden.

'I enjoy it very much,' she said. 'Very much. Such nice boys and girls . . .'

'Move along, kids,' Rollo said, walking by.

I nodded to Mrs Layden, moving along. 'Can you feature that?' Gloria asked. 'She ought to be home putting a diaper on the baby. Christ, I hope I never live to be that old.'

'How do you know those fellows are detectives?' I asked.

'I'm psychic,' Gloria replied. 'My God, can you feature that old lady? She's a nut about these things. They ought to charge her room rent.' She shook her head. 'I hope I never live to be that old,' she said again.

The meeting with the old lady depressed Gloria very much. She said it reminded her of the women in the little town in West Texas where she had lived.

'Alice Faye's just come in,' one of the girls said. 'See her? Sitting right over there.'

It was Alice Faye all right, with a couple of men I didn't recognize.

'See her?' I asked Gloria.

'I don't want to see her,' Gloria said.

'Ladies and gentlemen,' Rocky said into the microphone, 'we are honoured tonight to have with us that beautiful moving picture star, Miss Alice Faye. Give Miss Faye a big hand, ladies and gentlemen.'

Everybody applauded and Miss Faye nodded her head, smiling. Socks Donald, sitting in a box seat by the orchestra platform, was smiling too. The Hollywood crowd had started coming.

'Come on,' I said to Gloria, 'clap your hands.'

'Why should I applaud for her?' Gloria said. 'What's she got I haven't? . . .'

'You're jealous,' I said.

'You're goddam right I'm jealous. As long as I am a failure I'm jealous of anybody who's a success. Aren't you?'

'Certainly not,' I said.

'You're a fool,' she said.

'Hey, look,' I said.

The two detectives had left the box with Mrs Layden and were sitting with Socks Donald. They had their heads together, looking at a sheet of paper one of them was holding.

'All right, kids,' Rocky said in the microphone. 'A little sprint before the rest period . . . Give,' he said to the orchestra, clapping his hands together and stamping on the platform, keeping time to the music. In a moment the customers were clapping their hands together and stamping too.

We were all milling around in the middle of the floor, all of us watching the minute hand of the clock, when suddenly Kid Kamm of Couple No. 18 began slapping his partner on the cheek. He was holding her up with his left hand, slapping her backwards and forwards with his right hand. But she did not respond. She was dead to the world. She gurgled a couple of times and then slid to the floor, unconscious.

The floor judge blew his whistle and all the customers jumped to their feet, excited. Customers at a marathon dance do not have to be prepared for their excitement. When anything happens they get excited all at once. In that respect a marathon dance is like a bull fight.

The floor judge and a couple of nurses picked up the girl and carried her off, her toes dragging, to the dressing room.

'Mattie Barnes, of Couple No. 18, has fainted,' Rocky announced to the crowd. 'She has been taken to the dressing room, ladies and gentlemen, where she will have the best of medical attention. Nothing serious, ladies and gentlemen – nothing serious. It just proves that there's always something happening at the world's championship marathon dance.'

'She was complaining last rest period,' Gloria said.

'What's the matter with her?' I asked.

'It's that time of the month,' Gloria said. 'And she'll never be able to come back either. She's the type that has to go to bed for three or four days when she gets it.'

'Can I pick 'em,' said Kid Kamm. He shook his head, disgusted. 'Boy, am I hoodooed! I been in nine of these things and I ain't finished one yet. My partner always caves in on me.'

'She'll probably be all right,' I said, trying to cheer him up.

'Nope,' he said, 'she's finished. She can go back to the farm now.'

The siren blew, meaning it was the end of another grind. Everybody ran for the dressing rooms. I kicked off my shoes, piling on my cot. I felt the ocean surge once – just once. Then I was asleep.

I woke up, my nose full of ammonia. One of the trainers was moving a bottle across my chin letting me inhale it. (This was the best way to arouse one of us from a deep sleep, the doctor said. If they had tried to wake you up by shaking you, they never would have done it.)

'All right,' I said to the trainer. 'I'm all right.'

I sat up, reaching for my shoes. Then I saw those two detectives and Socks Donald standing near me, by Mario's cot. They were waiting for the other trainer to wake him up. Finally Mario rolled over, looking at them.

'Hello, buddy,' said one of the detectives. 'Know who this is?' He handed him a sheet of paper. Now I was close enough to see what it was. It was a page torn out of a detective magazine, containing several pictures.

Mario looked at it, then handed it back. 'Yeah, I know who it is,' he said, sitting up.

'You ain't changed much,' said the other detective.

'You wop son of a bitch,' Socks said, doubling his fist. 'What're you trying to pull on me?'

'Nix, Socks,' the first detective said. Then he spoke to Mario. 'Well, Giuseppe, get your things together.'

Mario started tying his shoes. 'I ain't got nothing but a coat and a toothbrush,' he said. 'But I would like to say good-bye to my partner.'

'You dirty wop son of a bitch,' Socks said. 'This'll look good in the newspapers, won't it?'

'Never mind your partner, Giuseppe,' the second detective said. 'Hey son,' he said to me, 'you tell Giuseppe's partner good-bye for him. Come on Giuseppe,' he said to Mario.

'Take that wop son of a bitch out the back way, boys,' said Socks Donald.

'Everybody on the floor,' yelled the floor judge. 'Everybody on the floor.'

'So long, Mario,' I said.

Mario did not say anything. It had all been very quiet, very matter-of-fact. These detectives acted as if this kind of thing happened every day.

. . . of which you have been
convicted by verdict of
the jury . . .

...*chapter six*

So, Mario went to jail and Mattie went back to the farm. *I remember how surprised I was when they arrested Mario for murder. I couldn't believe it. He was one of the nicest boys I'd ever met. But that was then that I couldn't believe it. Now I know you can be nice and be a murderer too. Nobody was ever nicer to a girl than I was to Gloria, but there came the time when I shot and killed her. So you see being nice doesn't mean a thing. . . .*

Mattie was automatically disqualified when the doctor refused to let her continue in the contest. He said if she did go on with the dance she would injure some of her organs and never be able to have a baby. She raised hell about it, Gloria said, calling the doctor a lot of names and absolutely refusing to quit. But she did quit. She had to. They had the axe over her.

That teamed her partner, Kid Kamm, with Jackie. Under the rules you could do that. You could solo for twenty-four hours but if you didn't get a partner by then you were disqualified. Both the Kid and Jackie seemed well satisfied with the new arrangement. Jackie had nothing to say about losing Mario. Her attitude was that a partner was a partner.

But the Kid was all smiles. He seemed to think that at last he had broken his hoodoo.

'They're liable to win,' Gloria said. 'They're strong as mules. That Alabama is corn-fed. Look at that beam. I bet she can go six months.'

'I'll string along with James and Ruby,' I said.

'After the way they've treated us?'

'What's that got to do with it? Besides, what's the matter with us? We've got a chance to win, haven't we?'

'Have we?'

'Well, you don't seem to think so,' I said.

She shook her head, not saying anything to that. 'More and more and more I wish I was dead,' she said.

There it was again. No matter what I talked about she always got back to that. 'Isn't there something I can talk about that won't remind you that you wish you were dead?' I asked.

'No,' she said.

'I give up,' I said.

Somebody on the platform turned the radio down. The music sounded like music now. (We used the radio all the time the orchestra wasn't there. This was in the afternoon. The orchestra came only at night.) 'Ladies and gentlemen,' Rocky said into the microphone, 'I have the honour to announce that two sponsors have come forward to sponsor two couples. The Pompadour Beauty Shop, of 415 Avenue B, will sponsor Couple No. 13 – James and Ruby Bates. Let's give the Pompadour Beauty Shop, of 415 Avenue B, a big hand for this, ladies and gentlemen – you too, kids. . . .

34

Everybody applauded.

'The second couple to be sponsored,' Rocky said, 'is No. 34, Pedro Ortego and Lillian Bacon. They are sponsored by the Oceanic Garage. All right, now, a big hand for the Oceanic Garage, located at 11,341 Ocean Walkway in Santa Monica.'

Everybody applauded again.

'Ladies and gentlemen,' Rocky said, 'there ought to be more sponsors for these marvellous kids. Tell your friends, ladies and gentlemen, and let's get sponsors for all the kids. Look at them, ladies and gentlemen, after 242 hours of continuous motion they are as fresh as daisies . . . a big hand for these marvellous kids, ladies and gentlemen.'

There was some more applause.

'And don't forget, ladies and gentlemen,' Rocky said, 'there's the Palm Garden right down there at the end of the hall where you can get delicious beverages – all kinds of beer and sandwiches. Visit the Palm Garden, ladies and gentlemen. . . . Give,' he said to the radio, turning the knob and filling the hall with noise again.

Gloria and I walked over to Pedro and Lillian. Pedro limped from a game leg. The story was that he had been gored in a bull ring in Mexico City. Lillian was a brunette. She too had been trying to get in the movies when she heard about the marathon dance.

'Congratulations,' I said.

'It proves somebody is for us,' Pedro said.

'As long as it couldn't be Metro-Goldwyn-Mayer it might as well be a garage,' Lillian said. 'Only it seems a little queer for a garage to be buying me underclothes.'

'Where do you get that underclothes stuff?' Gloria said. 'You don't get underclothes. You get a sweatshirt with the garage's name across the back of it.'

'I get underclothes, too,' Lillian said.

'Hey, Lillian,' said Rollo, the floor judge, 'the woman from the Oceanic Garage wants to talk to you.'

'The what? . . .' asked Lillian.

'Your sponsor, Mrs Yeargan – '

'For crying out loud,' said Lillian. 'Pedro, it looks like you get the underclothes.'

Gloria and I walked down by the master of ceremonies' platform. It was nice down there about this time of the afternoon. There was a big triangle of sunshine that came through the double window above the bar in the Palm Garden. It only lasted about ten minutes but during those ten minutes I moved slowly about in it (I had to move to keep from being disqualified) letting it cover me completely. It was the first time I had ever appreciated the sun. 'When this marathon is over,' I told myself, 'I'm going to spend the rest of my life in the sun. I can't wait to go to the Sahara Desert to make a picture.' *Of course, that won't ever happen now.*

I watched the triangle on the floor get smaller and smaller.

Finally it closed altogether and started up my legs. It crawled up my body like a living thing. When it got to my chin I stood on my toes, to keep my head in it as long as possible. l did not close my eyes. I kept them wide open, looking straight into the sun. It did not blind me at all. In a moment it was gone.

I looked around for Gloria. She was standing at the

platform, swaying from side to side, talking to Rocky, who was sitting on his haunches. Rocky was swaying too. (All the employees – the doctor, the nurses, the floor judges, the master of ceremonies, even the boys who sold soda pop – had been given orders to keep moving when they talked to one of the contestants. The management was very strict about this.)

'You looked very funny standing out there on your toes,' Gloria said. 'You looked like a ballet dancer.'

'You practise up on that and I'll let you do a solo,' Rocky said, laughing.

'Yes,' Gloria said. 'How was the sun today?'

'Don't let 'em kid you,' Mack Aston, of Couple No. 5, said as he passed by.

'Rocky!' a voice called. It was Socks Donald. Rocky got down from the platform and went to him.

'I don't think it's very nice of you to razz me,' I said to Gloria. 'I don't ever razz you.'

'You don't have to,' she said. 'I get razzed by an expert. God razzes me. . . . You know what Socks Donald wants with Rocky? You want some inside information?'

'What?' I asked.

'You know No. 6 – Freddy and that Manski girl. Her mother is going to prefer charges against him and Socks. She ran away from home.'

'I don't see what that's got to do with it,' I said.

'She's jail bait,' Gloria said. 'She's only about fifteen. God, with all of it running around loose it does look like a guy would have better sense.'

'Why blame Freddy? It may not be his fault.'

'According to the law it's his fault,' Gloria said. 'That's what counts.'

I steered Gloria back to where Socks and Rocky were standing, trying to overhear what was being said; but they were talking too low. Rather, Socks was doing all the talking. Rocky was listening, nodding his head.

'Right now,' I heard Socks say, and Rocky nodded that he understood and came back on the floor, winking wisely to Gloria as he passed. He went to Rollo Peters and called him aside, whispering earnestly for a few seconds. Then Rollo left, looking around, as if he were trying to find somebody, and Rocky went back to the platform.

'The kids only have a few minutes left before they retire for their well-earned rest period,' Rocky announced into the microphone. 'And while they are off the floor, ladies and gentlemen, the painters will paint the big oval on the floor for the derby tonight. The derby tonight, ladies and gentlemen: don't forget the derby. Positively the most thrilling thing you ever saw – all right, kids, two minutes to go before you retire – a little sprint, kids – show the ladies and gentlemen how fresh you are – You, too, ladies and gentlemen, show these marvellous kids you're behind them with a rally – '

He turned up the radio a little and began clapping his hands and stamping his foot. The audience joined in the rally. All of us stepped a little more lively, but it was not because of the rally. It was because within a minute or two we got a rest period and directly after that we were to be fed.

Gloria nudged me and I looked up to see Rollo Peters walking between Freddy and the Manski girl. I thought the Manski girl was crying, but before Gloria and I could catch up with them the siren blew and everybody made a dash for the dressing rooms.

Freddy was standing over his cot, stuffing an extra pair of shoes into a small zipper bag.

'I heard about it,' I said. 'I'm very sorry.'

'It's all right,' he said. 'Only she's the one who did the raping. . . . I'll be all right if I can get out of town before the cops pick me up. It's a lucky thing for me that Socks was tipped off.'

'Where are you going?' I asked.

'South, I guess. I've always had a yen to see Mexico. So long. . . .'

'So long,' I said.

He was gone before anybody knew it. As he went through the back door I had a glimpse of the sun glinting on the ocean. For a moment I was so astounded I could not move. I do not know whether I was the more surprised at really seeing the sun for the first time in almost three weeks or discovering the door. I went over to it, hoping the sun would not be gone when I got there. *The only other time I ever was this eager was one Christmas when I was a kid, the first year I was big enough to really know what Christmas was, and I went into the front room and saw the tree all lighted up.*

I opened the door. At the end of the world the sun was

sinking into the ocean. It was so red and bright and hot I wondered why there was no steam. *I once saw steam come out of the ocean. It was on the highway at the beach and some men were working with gun-powder. Suddenly, it exploded, setting them on fire. They ran and dived into the ocean. That was when I saw the steam.*

The colour of the sun had shot up into some thin clouds, reddening them. Out there where the sun was sinking the ocean was very calm, not looking like an ocean at all. It was lovely, lovely, lovely, lovely, lovely, lovely. Several people were fishing off the pier, not paying any attention to the sunset. They were fools. 'You need that sunset worse than you do fish,' I told them in my mind.

The door flew out of my hands, slamming shut with a bang like that of a cannon going off.

'Are you deaf?' a voice yelled in my ear. It was one of the trainers. 'Keep that door closed! You wanna be disqualified?'

'I was only watching the sun set,' I said.

'Are you nuts? You ought to be asleep. You need your sleep,' he said.

'I don't need any sleep,' I said. 'I feel fine. I feel better than I ever felt in my life.'

'You need your rest anyway,' he said. 'You only got a few minutes left. Get off your feet.'

He followed me across the floor to my cot. Now I could notice the dressing room didn't smell so good. I am very susceptible to unpleasant odours and I wondered why I hadn't noticed this smell before, the smell of too many men in a room. I kicked off my shoes and stretched out on my back.

'You want your legs rubbed?' he asked.

'I'm all right,' I said. 'My legs feel fine.'

He said something to himself and went away. I lay there, thinking about the sunset, trying to remember what colour it was. I don't mean the red, I mean the other shades. Once or twice I almost remembered; it was like a man you once had known but now had forgotten, whose size and letters and cadence you remembered but could not quite assemble.

Through the legs of my cot I could feel the ocean quivering against the pilings below. It rose and fell, rose and fell, went out and came back, went out and came back. . . .

I was glad when the siren blew, waking us up, calling us back to the floor.

. . . carrying with it the extreme penalty of the law . . .

...*chapter seven*

The painters had finished. They had painted a thick white line around the floor in the shape of an oval. This was the track for the derby.

'Freddy's gone,' I said to Gloria, as we walked to the table where the sandwiches and coffee had been set up. (This was called a light lunch. We had our big meal at ten o'clock at night.)

'So is the Manski girl,' Gloria said. 'Two welfare workers came and got her. I bet her old lady burns her cute little bottom.'

'I hate to say it,' I said, 'but Freddy's leaving was the brightest spot of my life.'

'What had he ever done to you?' she asked.

'Oh, I don't mean that,' I said. 'But if he hadn't left I wouldn't have got to see the sunset.'

'My God,' Gloria said, looking at her sandwich. 'Ain't there nothing in the world but ham?'

'To you that's turkey,' said Mack Aston, who was in line behind me. He was kidding.

'Here's a beef,' said the nurse. 'Would you rather have a beef?'

Gloria took the beef sandwich, but kept the ham too. 'Put four lumps in mine,' she said to Rollo, who was pouring the coffee. 'And lots of cream.'

'She's got a little horse in her,' said Mack Aston.

'Black,' I said to Rollo.

Gloria took her food over to the master of ceremonies' platform where the musicians were tuning up their instruments. When Rocky Gravo saw her he jumped down on the floor and began talking to her. There wasn't room there for me, so I went around to the opposite side.

'Hello,' said a girl. The shield on her back said: 7. She had black hair and black eyes and was rather pretty. I didn't know her name.

'Hello,' I said, looking around, trying to see whose partner she was. He was talking to a couple of women in a front row box.

'How are you making out?' No. 7 asked. Her voice sounded as if she had been well educated.

'What is she doing in this thing?' I asked myself. 'I guess I'm doing all right,' I replied. 'Only I wish it was all over and I was the winner.'

'What would you do with the money if you won?' she asked, laughing.

'I'd make a picture,' I said.

'You couldn't make much of a picture for a thousand dollars, could you?' she asked, taking a bite of her sandwich.

'Oh, I don't mean a big picture,' I explained. 'I mean a short. I could make a two-reeler for that, maybe three.'

'You interest me,' she said. 'I've been watching you for two weeks.'

'You have?' I said, surprised.

'Yes, I've seen you stand over there in the sun every afternoon and I've seen you with a thousand different expressions on your face. Sometimes I got the idea you were badly frightened.'

'You must be wrong,' I said. 'What's there to be frightened about?'

'I overheard what you said to your partner about seeing the sunset this afternoon,' she said, smiling.

'That doesn't prove anything,' I said.

'Suppose . . .' she said, glancing around. She looked at the clock, frowning. 'We've still got four minutes. Would you like to do something for me?'

'Well . . . sure,' I said.

She motioned with her head and I followed her behind the master of ceremonies' platform. This platform was about four feet high, draped with heavy, decorated canvas that fell to the floor. We were standing alone in a sort of cave that was formed by the back of the platform and a lot of signs. Except for the noise she and I might have been the only people left in the world. We were both a little excited.

'Come on,' she said. She dropped to the floor and lifted the canvas, crawling under the platform. My heart was beating rapidly and I felt the blood leave my face. Through the balls of my feet I could feel the ocean surging against the pilings below.

'Come on,' she whispered, pulling at my ankle. Suddenly

I knew what she meant. *There is no new experience in life. Something may happen to you that you think has never happened before, that you think is brand new, but you are mistaken. You have only to see or smell or hear or feel a certain something and you will discover that this experience you thought was new has happened before.* When she pulled at my ankle, trying to get me beneath the platform, I remembered the time when another girl had done exactly the same thing. Only it was a front porch instead of a platform. I was thirteen or fourteen years old then and the girl was about the same age. Her name was Mabel and she lived next door. After school we used to play under the front porch, imagining it was a cave and we were robbers and prisoners. Later we used it to play papa and mama, imagining it was a house. But on this day l am speaking of I stood by the front porch, not thinking of Mabel or games at all, and I felt something pulling at my ankle. I looked down and there was Mabel. 'Come on,' she said.

It was very dark under the platform and while I crouched there on my hands and knees trying to see through the gloom No. 7 suddenly grabbed me around the neck.

'Hurry . . .' she whispered.

'What's coming off here?' growled a man's voice. He was so close I could feel his breath against my hair. 'Who is that?'

I recognized the voice now. It was Rocky Gravo's. My stomach turned over. No. 7 let go my neck and slid out from under the platform. I was afraid if I tried to apologize or say anything Rocky would recognize my voice, so I quickly rolled under the curtain. No. 7 was already on her feet moving away, looking back over her shoulder at me. Her face was white as chalk. Neither of us spoke. We strolled onto the dance floor, trying to look very innocent. The nurse was collecting our dirty coffee cups in a basket. Then I discovered my hands and clothes were filthy with dust. I had a couple of minutes before the whistle blew, so I hurried into the dressing room to clean up. When that was done I felt better.

'What a close shave that was,' I told myself. 'I'll never do anything like that again.'

I got back on the floor as the whistle blew and the orchestra began to play. This was not a very good orchestra; but it was better than the radio because you didn't have to listen to a lot of announcers begging and pleading with you to buy something. Since I've been in this marathon I've had enough radio to last me the rest of my life. *There is a radio going now, in a building across the street from the court room. It is very distinct. 'Do you need money? . . . Are you in trouble? . . .'*

'Where've you been?' Gloria asked, taking my arm.

'I haven't been anywhere,' I said. 'Feel like dancing?'

'All right,' she said. We danced once around the floor and then she stopped. 'That's too much like work,' she said.

As I took my hand from around her waist I noticed my fingers were dirty again. 'That's funny,' I thought. 'I just washed them a minute ago.'

'Turn around,' I said to Gloria.

'What's the matter?' she asked.

'Turn around,' I said.

47

She hesitated, biting her lip, so I stepped behind her. She was wearing a white woollen skirt and a thin white woollen sweater. Her back was covered with thick dust and I knew where it had come from.

'What's the matter?' she said.

'Stand still,' I said. I brushed her off with my hand, knocking most of the dust and lint loose from her sweater and skirt. She did not speak for a moment or two. 'I must have got that when I was wrestling in the dressing room with Lillian,' she said finally.

'I'm not as big a sap as she thinks I am,' I told myself. 'I guess you did,' I said.

Rollo Peters fell in with us as we walked around the floor.

'Who is that girl?' I asked, pointing to No. 7.

'That's Guy Duke's partner. Her name is Rosemary Loftus.'

'All your taste is in your mouth,' Gloria said.

'I merely asked who she was,' I said. 'I haven't got a crush on her.'

'You don't need one,' Gloria said. 'You tell him, Rollo.'

'Leave me out of this,' Rollo said, shaking his head. 'I don't know a thing about her.'

'What about her?' I asked Gloria, as Rollo walked away, joining James and Ruby Bates.

'Are you that innocent?' she said. 'On the level – are you?' She laughed, shaking her head. 'You certainly are a card.'

'All right, forget it,' I said.

'Why, that dame is the biggest bitch west of the Mississippi River,' she said. 'She's a bitch with an exclusive education and when you get that kind of bitch you've got the worst bitch of all. Why not even the girls can go to the can when she's around – '

'Hello there, Gloria,' called out Mrs Layden. She was sitting in her usual seat in the front row box the far end of the hall, away from the master of ceremonies' platform. Gloria and I walked over to the railing. . . .

'How's my favourite couple?' she asked.

'Fine,' I said. 'How are you, Mrs Layden?'

'I'm fine too,' she said. 'I'm going to stay a long time tonight. See?' She pointed to her blanket and her lunch basket on the chair beside her. 'I'll be here to cheer you on.'

'We'll need it,' Gloria said.

'Why don't you take one of those boxes down there away from the Palm Garden?' I asked. 'It gets pretty rowdy at the bar later on when everybody starts drinking – '

'This is fine for me,' she said, smiling. 'I like to be here for the derby. I want to watch them make the turns. Would you like to see the afternoon paper?' she asked, pulling the paper out from under the blanket.

'Thank you,' I said. 'I would like to know what's going on in the world. How is the weather outside? Has the world changed much?'

'You're poking fun at me,' she said.

'No, I'm not . . . it just seems like I've been in this hall a million years. . . . Thanks for the paper, Mrs Layden. . . .'

As we moved away I unfolded the paper. Big, black headlines hit me in the face.

49

NAB YOUTHFUL MURDERER IN
MARATHON DANCE

Escaped Criminal Was Taking Part in Beach Contest

Detectives yesterday picked a murderer from the marathon dance now in progress on the amusement pier at Santa Monica. He was Giuseppe Lodi, 26-year-old Italian, who escaped eight months ago from the Illinois state prison at Joliet after serving four years of a fifty-year sentence for the conviction of the hold-up slaying of an aged druggist in Chicago.

Lodi entered in the marathon dance under the alias of Mario Petrone, offered no resistance when he was arrested by Detectives Bliss and Voight, of the Robbery Detail. The officers had dropped in to the marathon dance seeking diversion from their duties, they said, and recognized Lodi through a picture they said they had seen in 'The Line-Up', a department of a popular detective monthly which contains pictures and measurements of badly wanted criminals. . . .

'Can you beat that?' I said. 'I was right beside him when all that happened. I certainly feel sorry for Mario now.'

'Why,' said Gloria, 'what's the difference between us?'

Pedro Ortega, Mack Aston and a few others gathered around us, talking excitedly. I handed the paper to Gloria and walked on alone.

'That's a hell of a thing,' I thought. 'Fifty years! Poor Mario . . . *And when Mario hears the news about me, if he* ever does, he will think: "Poor guy! wasting his sympathy on me and him getting the rope. . . ."'"

At the next rest period Socks Donald had a surprise for us. He issued the uniforms we were to wear in the derby races; tennis shoes, white shorts, white sweat-shirts. All the boys were given thick leather belts to wear around their waists, and on either side of the belt were little handles, like those on luggage. These were for our partners to hold on when we went around the curves. It seemed very silly to me then, but later on I discovered Socks Donald knew what he was doing.

'Lissen, kids,' Socks said. 'Tonight we start on our first million. There'll be a lot of movie stars here for the derby and wherever they go the crowds will follow. Some team will lose tonight – some team will lose every night. I don't want no squawks about this because it's on the level. Everybody has the same chance. You'll get some extra time to get on your uniforms and some extra time to take them off. And by the way, I talked to Mario Petrone this afternoon. He told me to say good-bye to all his pals. Now, don't forget to give the customers a run for their money in the derby, kids – '

I was surprised to hear him mention Mario's name because the night before, when Mario was arrested, Socks had wanted to beat him up.

'I thought he was sore at Mario,' I said to Rollo.

'Not any more,' Rollo said. 'That was the best break we ever had. If it hadn't been for that nobody ever would have known there was a marathon dance. That newspaper publicity was just what the doctor ordered. Reservations have been coming in all afternoon.'

51

. . . you,
Robert Syverten,
be delivered . . .

...*chapter eight*

That night, for the first time since the contest started, the hall was crowded and practically every seat was taken. The Palm Garden was crowded too and there was a lot of boisterous laughing and talking at the bar. 'Rollo was right,' I said to myself. 'Mario's arrest was the best break Socks ever had.' (But not all those people had been attracted by the newspaper publicity. I found out later that Socks was having us advertised over several radio stations.)

We walked around in our track suits while the trainers and nurses set up the floor for the derby.

'I feel naked,' I said to Gloria.

'You look naked,' she said. 'You ought to have on a jock-strap.'

'They didn't give me one,' I said. 'Does it show that much?'

'It's not only that,' she said. 'You're liable to get ruptured. Get Rollo to buy you one tomorrow. They come in three sizes: small, medium and large. You take a small.'

'I'm not by myself,' I said, looking around at some of the other boys.

'They're bragging,' Gloria said.

Most of the contestants looked very funny in their track suits. I never saw such an odd assortment of arms and legs in my life.

'Look,' Gloria said, nodding to James and Ruby Bates. 'Ain't that something?'

You could see Ruby was going to have a baby. It looked as if she had stuffed a pillow under her sweat-shirt.

'It certainly is noticeable,' I said. 'But remember it's none of your business.'

'Ladies and gentlemen,' Rocky said into the microphone, 'before this sensational derby starts, I want to call your attention to the rules and regulations. Because of the number of contestants the derby will be run in two sections – forty couples in the first and forty in the second. The second derby will be run a few minutes after the first one and the entries in each one will be decided by drawing the numbers out of a hat.

'We'll run these derbies in two sections for a week, the couple in each one making the least number of laps to be eliminated. After the first week there will be only one derby. The kids will race around the track for fifteen minutes, the boys heeling and toeing, the girls trotting or running as they see fit. There is no prize for the winner, but if some of you ladies and gentlemen want to send up some prize money to encourage the kids, I know they will appreciate it.

'You will notice the cots in the middle of the floor, the nurses and trainers standing by with sliced oranges, wet towels, smelling salts and the doctor in charge to see that none of these kids carry on unless they're in good physical condition.'

The young doctor was standing in the middle of the floor, his stethoscope hanging from his neck, looking very important.

'Just a minute, ladies and gentlemen – just a minute,' Rocky said. 'I have in my hand a ten-dollar bill for the winner of tonight's derby, contributed by that marvellous little screen star, none other than Miss Ruby Keeler. A hand for Miss Keeler, ladies and gentlemen – '

Ruby Keeler stood up, bowing to the applause.

'That's the spirit, ladies and gentlemen,' Rocky said. 'And now we need some judges, ladies and gentlemen, to check the laps each couple makes. 'He stopped to wipe the perspiration off his face. 'All right now, ladies and gentlemen, I want these judges out of the audience – forty of them. Step right up here – don't be afraid – '

Nobody in the audience moved for a moment, and then Mrs Layden crawled under the railing and started across the floor. As she passed Gloria and me she smiled and winked.

'Maybe she'll turn out to be useful after all,' Gloria said.

Soon others followed Mrs Layden until all the judges had been selected. Rollo gave each of them a card and a pencil and seated them on the floor around the platform.

'All right, ladies and gentlemen,' Rocky said. 'We've got enough judges. Now we'll have the drawing for the first derby. There are eighty numbers in this hat and we'll draw forty of them. The other couples will be in the second derby. Now we need somebody to draw the numbers. How about you, lady?' he asked Mrs Layden, holding out the hat. Mrs Layden smiled and nodded her head.

'This is a big moment in her life,' Gloria said sarcastically.

'I think she is a very sweet old lady,' I said.

'Nuts,' Gloria said.

Mrs Layden began drawing out the numbers, passing them to Rocky, who announced them into the microphone.

'The first one,' he said, 'is Couple No. 105. Right over here, kids – all you couples who are drawn stand over here on this side of the platform.'

As fast as Mrs Layden would draw the numbers Rocky would announce them, then pass them to one of the judges. That was the couple he checked, counting the number of laps they made.

'. . . Couple No. 22,' Rocky said, handing the number to a young man who wore spectacles.

'Come on,' I said to Gloria. That was our number.

'I'd like that one,' I heard Mrs Layden say to Rocky. 'That's my favourite couple.'

'Sorry, lady,' Rocky said. 'You have to take them in order.'

When the drawing was finished and we were all together near the starting line, Rocky said, 'All right, ladies and gentlemen, we're almost ready. Now, kids, all you boys remember heel and toe. If one of you has to go to the pit for any reason whatsoever, your partner has to make two laps of the track to count for one. Will you start 'em off Miss Keeler?'

She nodded and Rocky handed Rollo the pistol. He took it to Miss Keeler, who was sitting in a front-row box with another girl I didn't recognize. Jolson was not there.

'All right, ladies and gentlemen, hold your hats,' Rocky

said. 'All right, Miss Keeler. . . .' He signalled to her with his hand.

Gloria and I had edged along the side of the platform towards the starting line and when Miss Keeler pulled the trigger we jumped away, pushing and shoving to get in front. Gloria had me by the arm.

'Hold on to the belt,' I yelled, struggling to get through the crowd. Everybody was stumbling over everybody else, trying to get in front . . . but in a minute we spread out and began pounding around the track. I was taking such long steps Gloria had to trot to keep up with me.

'Heel and toe there,' Rollo said. 'You're running.'

'I'm doing the best I can,' I said.

'Heel and toe,' he said 'Like this – '

He stepped in front of me, illustrating what he meant. I had no trouble at all in learning. The trick was to keep your shoulders and arms properly timed. I had no trouble at all in figuring that. It seemed to come to me naturally. It was so simple, I thought for a moment I must have done some heel and toe walking before. I couldn't remember it, so evidently I hadn't. I've got a marvellous memory.

We had been going about five minutes and were well up towards the front when I felt Gloria stop propelling herself; that is, she stopped travelling under her own power. I was dragging her. I felt as if she were trying to pull the belt through my stomach.

'Too fast?' I asked, slowing down.

'Yes,' she replied, almost out of breath.

One of the nurses slammed a wet bath towel around my

neck, almost knocking me off balance. 'Rub your face with it,' I said to Gloria. . . . Just then Couple No. 35 cut in front of us, trying to get into the turn first. The spurt was too much for the girl. She began to stagger, loosening her hold on his belt.

'Stand by No. 35,' yelled Rocky Gravo, but before a nurse or trainer could reach her she had fallen on her face, sliding a couple of feet across the floor. If I had been alone I could have sidestepped the body, but with Gloria hanging on me I was afraid if I dodged I would sling her off. (Making these turns with a girl hanging on you was like playing pop-the-whip.)

'Look out!' I yelled, but the warning was too late to do any good. Gloria stumbled over the body, pulling me down with her, and the next thing I knew four or five couples were piled together on the floor, struggling to get up. Rocky said something into the microphone and the crowd gasped.

I picked myself up. I wasn't hurt, only I knew from the way my knees were burning that all the skin was rubbed off. The nurses and trainers rushed over and began tugging at the girls, carrying Gloria and Ruby to the cots in the pit.

'Nothing serious, ladies and gentlemen,' Rocky said. 'Just a little spill . . . something happens every minute in the derbies . . . while the girls are in the pit the boys have to make two laps to count as one full lap for the team. All right, kids, give those solos the inside track.'

I began walking very fast so as not to lose our position in the race. Now that Gloria wasn't hanging on to the strap any more I felt light as a feather. A nurse and a trainer began working over her while the doctor listened to her heart with his stethoscope. The nurse was holding smelling salts at her nose and the trainer was massaging her legs. Another trainer and nurse were doing the same thing to Ruby. I made four laps before Gloria came back to the floor. She was very pale.

'Can you hold out?' I asked, slowing down. She said yes with her head. The people were applauding and stamping their feet and Rocky was speaking words into the microphone. Ruby came back into the race, looking all in too.

'Take it easy,' Rollo said, moving beside me. 'You're in no danger – '

Then I felt a sharp pain in my left leg that shot up through my body and almost blew off the top of my head. 'My God,' I told myself: 'I'm paralysed!'

'Kick it out, kick it out,' Rollo said.

I couldn't bend my leg. It simply wouldn't work. It was stiff as a board. Every time I took a step the pain went through the top of my head.

'There's a charley horse on Couple 22,' Rocky said into the microphone. 'Stand by there, trainers – '

'Kick it out, kick it out,' Rollo said.

I kicked my leg against the floor but that was more painful than ever.

'Kick it out, kick it out – '

'You son of a bitch,' I said; 'my leg hurts – '

Two of the trainers grabbed me by the arms and helped me to the pit.

'There goes the brave little girl of No. 22,' Rocky announced, 'little Gloria Beatty. What a brave kid she is!

59

She's soloing while her partner is in the pit with a charley horse – look at her burn up that track! Give her the inside, kids – '

One of the trainers held my shoulders down while the other one worked my leg up and down, beating the muscles with the heels of his fists.

'That hurts,' I said.

'Take it easy, said the trainer who was holding my shoulders. 'Didn't you ever have one of those things before?'

Then I felt something snap in my leg and the pain was suddenly gone.

'Okay,' the trainer said.

I got up, feeling fine, and went back on the track, standing there waiting for Gloria. She was on the opposite side from me, trotting, her head bobbing up and down every time she took a step. I had to wait for her to come around. (The rules were you had to come out of the pit at the point where you went in.) As Gloria neared me I started walking and in a moment she had coupled on to the belt.

'Two minutes to go,' Rocky announced. 'A little rally, ladies and gentlemen – ' They began clapping their hands and stamping their feet, much louder than before.

Other couples began to sprint past us and I put on a little more steam. I was pretty sure Gloria and I weren't in last place, but we had both been in the pit and I didn't want to take a chance on being eliminated. When the pistol sounded for the finish half the teams collapsed on the floor. I turned around to Gloria and saw her eyes were glassy. I knew she was going to faint.

'Hey . . .' I yelled to one of the nurses, but just then Gloria sagged and I had to catch her myself. It was all I could do to carry her to the pit. 'Hey!' I yelled to one of the trainers. 'Doctor!'

Nobody paid any attention to me. They were too busy picking up the bodies. The customers were standing on their seats, screaming in excitement.

I began rubbing Gloria's face with a wet towel. Mrs Layden suddenly appeared beside me and took a bottle of smelling salts off the table by the cot.

'You go to your dressing room,' she said. 'Gloria'll be all right in a minute. She's not used to the strain.'

I was on a boat going to Port Said. I was on my way to the Sahara Desert to make that picture. I was famous and I had plenty of money. I was the most important picture director in the world. I was more important than Sergei Eisenstein. The critics of *Vanity Fair* and *Esquire* had agreed that I was a genius. I was walking around the deck, thinking of that marathon dance I once had been in, wondering what had become of all those girls and boys, when something hit me a terrific blow in the back of the head, knocking me unconscious. I had a feeling I was falling.

When I struck the water I began lashing out with my arms and legs because I was afraid of sharks. Something brushed my body and I screamed in fright.

· I woke up swimming in water that was freezing cold. Instantly I knew where I was. 'I've had a nightmare,' I told myself. The thing that had brushed my body was a hundred-

pound block of ice. I was in a small tank of water in the
dressing room. I was still wearing my track suit. I climbed
out, shivering, and one of the trainers handed me a towel.

Two other trainers came in, carrying one of the contestants who was unconscious. It was Pedro Ortega. They
carried him to the tank and dumped him in.

'Is that what happened to me?' I asked.

'That's right,' the trainer said. 'You passed out just as
you left the dance floor – ' Pedro whimpered something in
Spanish and splashed the water, fighting to get out. The
trainer laughed. 'I'll say Socks knew what he was doing
when he brought that tank in here,' he said. 'That ice water
fixes 'em right up. Get off those wet pants and shoes.'

. . . by the
Sheriff of
Los Angeles
County
to the
Warden of
State Prison . . .

...*chapter nine*

The derby races were killing them off. Fifty-odd couples had been eliminated in two weeks. Gloria and I had come close to the finish once or twice, but by the skin of our teeth we managed to hang on. After we changed our technique we had no more trouble: we had stopped trying to win, not caring where we finished so long as it wasn't last.

We had got a sponsor too: Jonathan Beer, Non-Fattening. This came just in time. Our shoes were worn out and our clothes were ragged. Mrs Layden sold Jonathan Beer on the idea of sponsoring us. *Sell St Peter on the idea of letting me in, Mrs Layden. I think I'm on my way.* They gave Gloria and me three pairs of shoes, three pairs of grey flannel trousers and three sweaters each with their product advertised on the backs of them.

I had gained five pounds since the contest started and was beginning to think that maybe we had some chance to win that thousand dollar first prize after all. But Gloria was very pessimistic.

'What are you going to do after this thing is over?' she asked.

'Why worry about that?' I said: 'It's not over yet. I don't see what you're kicking about,' I told her. 'We're better off than we've ever been – at least we know where our next meal is coming from.'

'I wish I was dead,' she said. 'I wish God would strike me dead.'

She kept saying that over and over again. It was beginning to get on my nerves.

'Some day God is going to do that little thing,' I said.

'I wish He would . . . I wish I had the guts to do it for Him.'

'If we win this thing you can take your five-hundred dollars and go away somewhere,' I said. 'You can get married. There are always plenty of guys willing to get married. Haven't you ever thought about that?'

'I've thought about it plenty,' she said. 'But I couldn't ever marry the kind of man I want. The only kind that would marry me would be the kind I wouldn't have. A thief or a pimp or something.'

'I know why you're so morbid,' I said. 'You'll be all right in a couple of days. You'll feel better about it then.'

'That hasn't got anything to do with it,' she said.

'I don't even get a backache from that. That's not it. This whole business is a merry-go-round. When we get out of here we're right back where we started.'

'We've been eating and sleeping,' I said.

'Well, what's the good of that when you're just postponing something that's bound to happen?'

65

'Hey, Jonathan Beer,' Rocky Gravo called out. 'Come over here – '

He was standing by the platform with Socks Donald. Gloria and I went over.

'How'd you kids like to pick up a hundred bucks?' Rocky asked.

'Doing what?' Gloria asked.

'Well, kids,' Socks Donald said, 'I've got a swell idea only I need a bit of some help – '

'That's the Ben Bernie influence,' Gloria said to me.

'What?' Socks said.

'Nothing,' Gloria said. 'Go on – you need a bit of some help – '

'Yeah,' Socks said. 'I want you two kids to get married here. A public wedding.'

'Married?' I said.

'Now, wait a minute,' Socks said. 'It's not that bad. I'll give you fifty dollars apiece and after the marathon is over you can get divorced if you want to. It don't have to be permanent. It's just a showmanship angle. What do you say?'

'I say you're nuts,' Gloria said.

'She doesn't mean that, Mr Donald – ' I said.

'The hell I don't,' she said. 'I've got no objection to getting married,' she said to Socks, 'but why don't you pick out Gary Cooper or some big-shot producer or director? I don't want to marry this guy. I got enough trouble looking out for myself – '

'It don't have to be permanent,' Rocky said. 'It's just showmanship.'

'That's right,' Socks said. 'Of course, the ceremony'll have to be on the square – we'll have to do that to get the crowd. But – '

'You don't need a wedding to get a crowd,' Gloria said. 'You're hanging 'em off the rafters now. Ain't it enough of a show to see those poor bastards falling all over the floor every night?'

'You don't get the angle,' Socks said, frowning.

'The hell I don't,' Gloria said. 'I'm way ahead of you.'

'You want to get in pictures and here's your chance,' Socks said. 'I already got some stores lined up to give you your wedding dress and your shoes and a beauty shop that'll fix you up – there'll be a lot of directors and supervisors here and they'll all be looking at nobody but you. It's the chance of a lifetime. What do you say, kid?' he asked me.

'I don't know – ' I said, not wanting to make him sore. After all, he was the promoter. I knew if he got sore at us we were as good as disqualified.

'He says no,' Gloria said.

'She does his thinking for him,' Rocky said sarcastically.

'Okay,' Socks said, shrugging his shoulders. 'If you can't use a hundred dollars maybe some of these other kids can. At least,' he said to me, 'you know who wears the drawers in your family.' He and Rocky both laughed.

'You just can't be polite to anybody, can you?' I said to Gloria when we had walked away. 'We'll be out in the street any minute now.'

'Might as well be now as tomorrow,' she said.

'You're the gloomiest person I ever met,' I said. 'Sometimes I think you would be better off dead,'

'I know it,' she said.

When we came around by the platform again I saw Socks and Rocky talking earnestly to Vee Lovell and Mary Hawley, Couple No. 71.

'Looks like Socks is selling her a bill of goods,' Gloria said. 'That Hawley horse couldn't get in out of the rain.'

James and Ruby Bates joined up and we walked four abreast. We were on friendly terms again since Gloria had stopped trying to talk Ruby into having an abortion performed. 'Did Socks proposition you to get married?' Ruby asked.

'Yes,' I said. 'How did you know?'

'He's propositioned everybody,' she said.

'We turned him down cold,' Gloria said.

'A public wedding isn't so bad,' Ruby said. 'We had one – '

'You did?' I said, surprised. James and Ruby were so dignified and quiet and so much in love with each other I couldn't imagine them being married in a public ceremony.

'We were married in a marathon dance in Oklahoma,' she said. 'We got about three hundred dollars worth of stuff too. . . .'

'Her old man gave us the shotgun for a wedding present – ' James said, laughing.

Suddenly a girl screamed behind us. We turned around. It was Lillian Bacon, Pedro Ortega's partner. She was walking backwards, trying to get away from him. Pedro caught up with her, slamming her in the face with his fist.

She sat down on the floor, screaming again. Pedro grabbed her by the throat with both hands, choking her and trying to lift her up. His face was the face of a maniac. There was no doubt he was trying to kill her.

Everybody started running for him at the same time. There was a lot of confusion.

James and I reached him first, grabbing him and breaking his hold on Lillian's neck. She was sitting on the floor, her body rigid, her arms behind her, her head thrown back, her mouth open – like a patient in a dentist's chair.

Pedro was muttering to himself and did not seem to recognize any of us. James shoved him and he staggered backward. I put my hands under Lillian's armpits, helping her to her feet. She was shaking like a muscle dancer.

Socks and Rocky rushed up and took Pedro by either arm. 'What's the big idea?' Socks roared.

Pedro looked at Socks, moving his lips but not saying anything. Then he saw Rocky and the expression on his face changed, becoming one of ferocious resentment. He suddenly twisted his arms free, stepping backward and reaching into his pocket.

'Look out – ' somebody cried.

Pedro lunged forward, a knife in his hand. Rocky tried to dodge, but it all happened so quickly he never had a chance. The knife caught him across the left arm two inches below the shoulder. He yelled and started running. Pedro turned around to follow but before he could take a step Socks hit him in the back of the head with a leather blackjack. You could hear the plunk above the music of the radio. It sounded exactly like somebody thumping their finger against a watermelon. Pedro stood there, an idiotic grin on his face and Socks hit him again with the blackjack.

Pedro's arms fell and the knife dropped to the floor. He wobbled on his legs and then he went down.

'Get him out of here,' Socks said, picking up the knife.

James Bates, Mack Aston and Vee Lovell lifted Pedro, carrying him off to the dressing room.

'Keep your seats, ladies and gentlemen – ' Socks said to the audience. 'Please – '

I was bracing Lillian from behind. She was still shaking.

'What happened?' Socks asked her.

'He accused me of cheating – ' she said. 'Then he hit me and started choking me – '

'Go on, kids,' Socks said. 'Act like nothing has happened. Hey, nurse – help this girl to the dressing room – ' Socks signalled to Rollo on the platform and the siren blew for a rest period. It was a few minutes early. The nurse took Lillian out of my arms and all the girls gathered around them, going into the dressing room.

As I went off I could hear Rollo making some kind of casual announcement over the loud speakers.

Rocky was standing at the wash basin, his coat and shirt off, dabbing at his shoulder with a handful of paper towels. The blood was streaming down his arm, running off his fingers.

'You better get the doctor on that,' Socks said. 'Where the hell is that doctor?' he bellowed.

'Here – ' the doctor said, coming out of the lavatory.

'The only time we need you you're sitting on your fanny,' Socks said. 'See what's the matter with Rocky.'

Pedro was lying on the floor with Mack Aston straddling him, working on his stomach like a lifeguard with a man who had been drowning.

'Watch it – ' Vee Lovell said, coming up with a bucket of water. Mack stepped back and Vee dumped the water in Pedro's face. It had no effect on him. He lay there like a log.

James Bates brought another bucket of water and doused him with that. Now Pedro began to show signs of life. He stirred, opening his eyes.

'He's coming to,' Vee Lovell said.

'I better get Rocky to the hospital in my car,' the doctor said, taking off his linen coat. 'He's got a deep cut – almost to the bone. It'll have to be sutured. Who did it?'

'That bastard – ' Socks said, pointing to Pedro with his leg.

'He must have used a razor,' the doctor said.

'Here – ' Socks said, handing him the knife. Socks had the leather blackjack in his other hand, the thong still around his wrist.

'Same thing,' the doctor said, handing back the knife.

Pedro sat up, rubbing his jaw, a dazed look on his face.

'It isn't your jaw,' I said to him in my mind, 'it was the back of your head.'

'For Christ's sake, let's get going,' Rocky said to the doctor. 'I'm bleeding like a stuck pig. And you, you son of a bitch,' he said to Pedro; 'I'm going to prefer charges against you – '

Pedro looked at him fiercely, saying nothing.

'There won't be any charges filed,' Socks said. 'I'm having enough trouble keeping open now. Next time be careful who you cheat with.'

'I wasn't cheating anybody,' Rocky said.

' – ' Socks said. 'Take him out the back way, Doc.'

'All right, Rocky,' the doctor said. Rocky started out. The temporary gauze bandage on his arm was soaked already. The doctor draped a coat around Rocky's shoulders and they went out.

'Are you trying to bust up this contest?' Socks asked, turning his full attention to Pedro. 'Whyn't you wait till this was over to get him?'

'I tried to cut his throat,' Pedro stated calmly, in precise English. 'He seduced my fiancée – '

'If he seduced your fiancée around here he's a magician,' Socks said. 'There's no place to seduce anybody.'

'I know a place,' I said in my mind.

Rollo Peters came into the dressing room. 'You guys ought to be getting your sleep,' he said. 'Where's Rocky?' he asked, looking around.

'The doc took him to hospital,' Socks told him. 'How are they out there?'

'They're calmed down,' Rollo said. 'I told 'em we were rehearsing a novelty act. What was the matter with Rocky?'

'Nothing much,' Socks said. 'He just damn near had his arm cut off by this greaseball, that's all.' He handed him Pedro's knife. 'Here take this thing and get rid of it. You do the announcing till we find out about Rocky.'

72

Pedro got up off the floor. 'I am very sorry I have a very quick temper – '

'I guess it could have been worse,' Socks said. 'It could have happened at night when we had a full house. How's your head?'

'It is sore,' Pedro said. 'I am very sorry this happened. I wanted to win the thousand dollars – '

'You still got a chance,' Socks said.

'You mean I am not disqualified? You mean you forgive me?'

'I forgive you – ' Socks said, dropping the blackjack into his pocket.

. . . to be
by said
Warden . . .

...*chapter ten*

'Ladies and gentlemen,' Rocky announced, 'before the derby starts the management has asked me to tell you that there will be a public wedding here one week from tonight – a real, bona-fide wedding right here on the floor between Couple No. 71, Vee Lovell and Mary Hawley. Step out there, Vee and Mary, and let the ladies and gentlemen see what a cute couple you are – '

Vee and Mary, in track suits, went to the centre of the floor, bowing to the applause. The hall was packed again.

' – That is,' Rocky said, 'if they are not eliminated in the derby by then. We hope not, anyway. This public wedding is in line with the management's policy to give you nothing but high-class entertainment – '

Mrs Layden tugged at the back of my sweatshirt.

'What's the matter with Rocky's arm?' she asked in a whisper. You could see Rocky had had some kind of an accident. His right arm was through his coat sleeve in the usual way, but his left arm was in a sling and on that side he wore his coat like a cape.

'He sprained it,' I said.

'They only took nine stitches in it,' Gloria said, under her breath.

'That's why he wasn't here last night,' Mrs Layden said. 'He had an accident – '

'Yes'm – '

'Did he fall?'

'Yes'm, I think so – '

' – introducing that beautiful screen star Miss Mary Brian. Will you take a bow, Miss Brian?'

Miss Brian took a bow. The audience applauded.

' – and that master comedian, Mr Charley Chase – '

There was more applause as Charley Chase stood up in a box seat and took a bow.

'I hate these introductions,' Gloria said.

'Good luck – ' Mrs Layden said as we moved towards the platform.

'I'm sick of this,' Gloria said. 'I'm sick of looking at celebrities and I'm sick of doing the same thing over and over again – '

'Sometimes I'm sorry I ever met you,' I said. 'I don't like to say a thing like that, but it's the truth. Before I met you I didn't know what it was to be around gloomy people.'

We crowded behind the starting line with the other couples.

'I'm tired of living and I'm afraid of dying,' Gloria said.

'Say, that's a swell idea for a song,' said James Bates, who had overheard her. 'You could write a song about an old nigger down on the levee who was tired of living and afraid of dying. He could be heaving cotton and singing a song to the Mississippi River. Say, that's a good title – you could call it Old Man River – '

Gloria looked daggers at him, thumbing her nose.

'Hello, there – ' Rocky called out to Mrs Layden, who had arrived at the platform. 'Ladies and gentlemen – ' he said into the microphone, 'I want to introduce to you the champion marathon dance fan of the world – a woman who hasn't missed a single night since this contest started. This is Mrs Layden, and the management has issued a season pass to her – good any time, good all the time. A big hand for Mrs Layden, ladies and gentlemen. Will you take a bow, Mrs Layden – '

Mrs Layden hesitated a moment, badly rattled, not knowing exactly what she should do or say. But as the audience applauded she took a couple of steps forward, bowing awkwardly. You could see this was one of the biggest surprises of her life.

'You people who are dance fans have seen her here before,' Rocky said. 'She is a judge in the derby every night – we couldn't have a derby unless she was here. How do you like the marathon dance, Mrs Layden?' he asked, stooping down on his haunches and moving the microphone so she could talk into it.

'She hates it,' Gloria said under her breath. 'She wouldn't come to one on a bet, you dumb bastard – '

'I like it,' Mrs Layden said. She was so nervous she could hardly speak.

'Who's your favourite couple, Mrs Layden?'

'My favourite couple is No. 22 – Robert Syverten and Gloria Beatty.'

'Her favourite couple is No. 22, ladies and gentlemen, sponsored by Jonathan Non-Fattening Beer – You're pulling for them to win, are you, Mrs Layden?'

'Yes, I am and if I were younger, I'd be in this contest myself.'

'That's fine. Thank you very much, Mrs Layden. All right – and now it gives me pleasure to present you with a season pass, Mrs Layden – the gift of the management. You can come in any time without paying – '

Mrs Layden took the pass. She was so overwhelmed with gratitude and emotion that she was smiling and crying and nodding her head at the same time.

'That's another big moment,' Gloria said.

'Shut up!' I said.

'All right – are the judges ready?' Rocky asked, straightening up.

'All ready,' said Rollo, helping Mrs Layden to a chair in the judges' row.

'Ladies and gentlemen,' Rocky announced, 'most of you are familiar with the rules and regulations of the derby – but for the benefit of those who are seeing their first contest of this kind, I will explain so they will know what is going on. The kids race around the track for fifteen minutes, the boys heeling and toeing, the girls running or trotting as they so desire. If for any reason whatsoever one of them goes in the pit – the pit is in the centre of the floor where the iron cots are – if for any reason one of them goes in the pit, the partner has to make two laps of the track to count for one. Is that clear?'

'Get going,' somebody in the audience yelled.

'Are the nurses and trainers ready? Is the doctor standing by? All right – ' He handed the starter's pistol down to Rollo. 'Will you start the kids off, Miss Delmar?' Rocky asked into the microphone. 'Ladies and gentlemen, Miss Delmar is a famous Hollywood author and novelist – '

Rollo took the pistol to Miss Delmar.

'Hold your hats, ladies and gentlemen,' Rocky sang out. 'Orchestra, get ready to give. All right, Miss Delmar – '

She shot the pistol and we were off.

Gloria and I let the racehorses set the pace. We made no effort to get up in front. Our system was to set a steady clip and hold it. There was no special prize money tonight. Even if there had been it would have made no difference to us.

The audience applauded and stamped their feet, begging for thrills, but this was one night they didn't get them. Only one girl, Ruby Bates, went into the pit and that was only for two laps. And for the first time in weeks nobody collapsed on the floor when the race was over.

But something had happened that frightened me. Gloria had pulled on my belt harder and longer than she ever had before. For the last five minutes of the derby it seemed she had no power of her own. I had practically dragged her around the track. I had a feeling we had just missed being eliminated ourselves. *We had just missed. Later that night Mrs Layden told me she had spoken to the man who had checked us. We had made only two more laps than the losers. That chilled me. I made up my mind then that from now on I had better forget my system and open up.*

The losers were Basil Gerard and Geneva Tomblin, Couple No. 16. They were automatically disqualified. I knew Geneva was glad it was over. Now she could get married to the Captain of that live bait boat she had met during the first week of the contest.

Geneva came back on the floor while we were eating. She was dressed for the street and carried a small grip.

'Ladies and gentlemen – ' Rocky said into the microphone ' – there's that marvellous kid who was eliminated tonight. Doesn't she look pretty? A big hand, ladies and gentlemen – '

The audience applauded and Geneva bowed from side to side as she walked towards the platform.

'That's sportsmanship, ladies and gentlemen – she and her partner lost a hard-fought derby, but she is smiling – I'll let you in on a little secret, ladies and gentlemen – ' he moved his face closer to the microphone and whispered loudly: 'She's in love – she's going to get married. Yes, sir, ladies and gentlemen, the old marathon dance is the original home of romance, because Geneva is marrying a man she met right in this hall. Is he in the house, Geneva? Is he here?'

Geneva nodded, smiling.

'Where is the lucky man?' Rocky asked. 'Where is he? Stand up, skipper, and take a bow – '

Everybody in the audience craned their necks, looking around.

'There he is – ' Rocky shouted, pointing to the opposite end of the hall. A man had stepped over the railing from the box and was walking down the floor towards Geneva. He had the peculiar walk of a sailor.

'Say a word, skipper – ' Rocky said, tilting the microphone stand over.

'I fell in love with Geneva the first time I saw her,' the skipper said to the audience, 'and a couple of days later I asked her to quit the marathon dance and marry me. But she said, no, she didn't want to let her partner down; and there wasn't nothing for me to do but stick around. Now I'm glad she's disqualified and I can hardly wait for the honeymoon – '

The audience rocked with laughter. Rocky pulled the microphone stand upright again. 'A silver shower for the new bride, ladies and gentlemen – '

The skipper grabbed the stand, yanked the microphone down to his mouth. 'Never mind any contributions, folks,' he said. 'I guess I'm plenty able to take care of her – '

'The original Popeye,' Gloria said.

There was no silver shower. Not a single coin hit the floor.

'You see how modest he is,' Rocky said 'But I guess it's all right for me to tell you he is the captain of the Pacific Queen, an old four-master that's now a live bait barge anchored three miles off the pier. There are water taxis every hour during the day – and if any of you folks want some good deep-sea fishing go out with the skipper – '

'Kiss her, you chump,' somebody in the audience yelled.

The skipper kissed Geneva, then steered her off the floor while the audience howled and applauded.

'That's the second wedding the marathon dance has arranged, ladies and gentlemen,' Rocky announced. 'Don't forget our big public ceremony here next week when Couple No. 71, Vee Lovell and Mary Hawley, will get married right before your very eyes. Give – ' he said to the orchestra.

Basil Gerard came out of the dressing room in his street clothes and went to the table to get his last meal on the house.

Rocky sat down on the platform, swinging his legs off.

'Look out for my coffee – ' Gloria said.

'Okay, okay,' Rocky said, moving the cup a little. 'How's the food?'

'All right,' I said.

Two middle-aged women came up to us. I had seen them several times before, sitting in box seats. 'Are you the manager?' one of them asked Rocky.

'Not exactly,' Rocky said. 'I'm the assistant manager. What was it you wanted?'

'I'm Mrs Higby,' the woman said. 'This is Mrs Witcher. Could we talk to you in private?'

'This is private as any place I got,' Rocky said. 'What was it you wanted?'

'We are the president and the vice-president – '

'What's the matter?' asked Socks Donald, coming around behind me.

'This is the manager,' Rocky said, looking relieved.

The two women looked at Socks. 'We are the president and the vice-president of the Mothers' League for Good Morals – '

'Aw-aw,' Gloria said, under her breath.

'Yes?'

'We have a resolution for you,' Mrs Higby said, thrusting a folded paper into his hand.

'What's this all about?' Socks asked.

'Simply this,' Mrs Higby said. 'Our Good Morals League has condemned your contest – '

'Wait a minute,' Socks said. 'Let's go to my office and talk this thing over – '

Mrs Higby looked at Mrs Witcher, who nodded. 'Very well,' she said.

'You kids come along – you too, Rocky. Hey nurse – take these cups and plates away – ' He smiled at the two women. 'You see,' he said, 'we don't let the kids do anything that would waste their energy. This way, ladies – '

He led the way off the floor behind the platform to his office, in a corner of the building. As we walked along Gloria pretended to stumble, falling heavily against Mrs Higby, grabbing her around the head with her arms.

'Oh, I beg your pardon – I'm sorry – ' Gloria said, looking on the floor to see what she had stumbled over.

Mrs Higby said nothing, looking fiercely at Gloria, straightening her hat. Gloria nudged me, winking behind Mrs Higby's back.

83

'Remember, you kids are witnesses – ' Socks whispered as we went into his office. This office had formerly been a lounge and was very small. I noticed there had been very little change in it since the day Gloria and I had come here to make entries for the marathon. The only change was two more pictures of nude women Socks had tacked on the wall. Mrs Higby and Mrs Witcher spotted that instantly, exchanging significant looks.

'Sit down, ladies,' Socks said. 'What is it, now?'

'The Mothers' League for Good Morals has condemned your contest,' Mrs Higby said. 'We have decided it is low and degrading and a pernicious influence in the community. We have decided you must close it – '

'Close it?'

'At once. If you refuse we shall go to the City Council. This contest is low and degrading – '

'You got me all wrong, ladies,' Socks said. 'There's nothing degrading about this contest. Why, these kids love it. Every one of them has gained weight since it started – '

'You have a girl in this contest who is about to become a mother,' Mrs Higby said, 'one Ruby Bates. It is criminal to have that girl running and walking all day when her baby is about to be born. Moreover, it is shocking to see her exhibiting herself to the world in that half-dressed condition. I should think she at least would have the decency to wear a coat – '

'Well, ladies,' Socks said, 'I never looked at that angle before. Ruby always seemed to know what she was doing –

and I never paid no attention to her stomach. But I can see your point. You want me to put her out of the contest?'

'Most certainly,' Mrs Higby said. Mrs Witcher nodded her head.

'All right, ladies,' Socks said, 'anything you say. I'm not hard to do business with. I'll even pay her hospital bills. . . . Thanks for telling me about it. I'll take care of that right away – '

'That isn't all,' Mrs Higby said. 'Do you plan to have a public wedding next week or was that merely an announcement to draw a crowd of morons?'

'I never pulled nothing phony in my life,' Socks said. 'That wedding is on the level. I wouldn't double-cross my customers like that. You can ask anybody I do business with what kind of a guy I am – '

'We are familiar with your reputation,' Mrs Higby said. 'But even at that I can hardly believe you intend to sponsor a sacrilege like that – '

'The kids who are going to get married are very much in love with each other,' Rocky said.

'We won't permit such mockery,' Mrs Higby said. 'We demand that you close this contest immediately!'

'What'll happen to these kids if he does?' Gloria asked. 'They'll go right back on the streets – '

'Don't try to justify this thing, young woman,' Mrs Higby said. 'This contest is vicious. It attracts the bad element. One of your participants was an escaped murderer – that Chicago Italian – '

'Well, ladies, you surely don't blame me for that,' Socks said.

'We certainly do. We are here because it is our duty to keep our city clean and free from all such influences – '

'Do you mind if me and my assistant go outside to talk this over?' Socks asked. 'Maybe we can figure this out – '

'. . . Very well,' Mrs Higby said.

Socks motioned to Rocky and they went outside.

'Do you ladies have children of your own?' Gloria asked, when the door had closed.

'We both have grown daughters,' Mrs Higby said.

'Do you know where they are tonight and what they're doing?'

Neither woman said anything.

'Maybe I can give you a rough idea,' Gloria said. 'While you two noble characters are here doing your duty by some people you don't know, your daughters are probably in some guy's apartment, their clothes off, getting drunk.'

Mrs Higby and Mrs Witcher gasped in unison.

'That's generally what happens to the daughters of reformers,' Gloria said. 'Sooner or later they all get laid and most of 'em don't know enough to keep from getting knocked up. You drive 'em away from home with your goddam lectures on purity and decency, and you're too busy meddling around to teach 'em the facts of life – '

'Why – ' said Mrs Higby, getting red in the face.

'I – ' Mrs Witcher said.

'Gloria – ' I said.

'It's time somebody got women like you told,' Gloria said, moving over and standing with her back to the door, as if to keep them in, 'and I'm just the baby to do it. You're the kind of bitches who sneak in the toilet to read dirty books and tell filthy stories and then go out and try to spoil somebody else's fun – '

'You move away from that door, young woman, and let us out of here!' Mrs Higby shrieked. 'I refuse to listen to you. I'm a respectable woman. I'm a Sunday School teacher – '

'I don't move a —— inch until I finish,' Gloria said.

'Gloria – '

'Your Morals League and your goddam women's clubs,' she said, ignoring me completely, ' – filled with meddlesome old bitches who haven't had a —— in twenty years. Why don't you old dames go out and buy a —— once in a while? That's all that's wrong with you. . . .'

Mrs Higby advanced on Gloria, her arm raised as if to strike her.

'Go on – hit me,' Gloria said, not moving. 'Hit me! – You even touch me and I'll kick your head off!'

The door opened, bumping Gloria away from it. Socks and Rocky came in.

'This – this – ' Mrs Higby said, shaking her finger at Gloria.

'Don't stutter,' Gloria said, ' – say it. You know how to say the word. Whore. W-h-o-'

'Pipe down!' Socks said. 'Ladies, me and my assistant have decided to take any suggestions you have to offer – '

'Our suggestion is you close this place at once!' Mrs Higby said. 'Else we shall go to the City Council in the morning – '

She started out, followed by Mrs Witcher.

87

'Young woman,' Mrs Higby said to Gloria, 'you ought to be in a reform school!'

'I was in one once,' Gloria said. 'There was a dame just like you in charge. She was a lesbian. . . .'

Mrs Higby gasped again and went out, followed by Mrs Witcher.

Gloria slammed the door behind them, then sat down in a chair and began sobbing. She covered her face with her hands and tried to fight it off, but it was no use. She slowly leaned forward in the chair, bending double, shaking and twitching with emotion, as if she had completely lost control of the upper half of her body. For a full moment the only sounds in the room were her sobs and the rise and fall of the ocean which came through the half-raised window.

Then Socks went over and laid his hand tenderly on Gloria's head, 'Nix, kid, nix – ' he said.

'Keep all this under your hat,' Rocky said to me. 'Don't say anything to the others – '

'I won't,' I said. 'Does this mean we'll have to close up?'

'I don't think so,' Socks said. 'It just means we'll have to try to grease somebody. I'll talk to my lawyer in the morning. In the meantime, Rocky – break the news to Ruby. She's got to quit. A lot of women have been squawking about her – ' He looked at the door. 'I should have stuck to my own racket,' he said 'Goddam bastard women . . .

. . . executed
and put
to death . . .

...*chapter eleven*

MARATHON DANCE WAR STILL RAGES

Mothers' League Threatens
Mass Meeting Unless City
Council Will Close Contest

IS THIRD DAY OF CONTROVERSY

The Mothers' League for Good Morals continued their war on the marathon dance today, threatening to take the issue directly to the citizens themselves unless the City Council closes the contest. The marathon dance has been in progress at a beach resort for the past 36 days.

Mrs J. Franklin Higby and Mrs William Wallace Witcher, president and first vice-president of the Morals League, appeared before the City Council again this afternoon, protesting the continuance of the dance. They were told by the Council that the City Attorney was making a thorough study of the law to determine what legal steps could be taken.

'We can't take any action until we know how the law reads,' Tom Hinsdell, Council chief, said. 'So far we have failed to find any specific statute that covers this case, but the City Attorney is examining all the codes.'

'Would the City Council hesitate if a plague threatened our city?' Mrs Higby said. 'Certainly it wouldn't. If there are no specific laws to fit this situation let them pass emergency laws. The marathon dance is a plague – it is low and degrading and in the same hall there is a public bar that is a rendezvous for gangsters, racketeers and notorious criminals. Surely this is not the proper atmosphere for children. . . .'

I handed the newspaper back to Mrs Layden. 'Mr Donald told us his lawyer said the city couldn't do anything,' I said.

'That doesn't make much difference,' Mrs Layden said. 'Those women are out to close it and, law or no law, they'll do it.'

'I don't see any harm in the marathon,' I said, 'but they're right about the bar. I've seen a lot of tough characters in the Palm Garden. . . . How long do you think it'll take them to close us up?'

'I don't know,' she said. 'But they'll close it. What are you going to do then?'

'The first thing I'm going to do is get a lot of sun,' I said. 'I used to love the rain and hate the sun, but now it's the other way around. You don't get much sun in here – '

'After that what are you going to do?'

'I haven't made any plans,' I said.

91

'I see. Where's Gloria?'

'She's putting on her track suit. She'll be out in a minute.'

'She's beginning to weaken, isn't she? The doctor said he had to look at her heart several times a day.'

'That doesn't mean anything,' I said. 'He looks at all of them. Gloria's all right.'

Gloria wasn't all right and I knew it. We were having a lot of trouble with the derbies. I never will know how we got by the last two nights. Gloria was in and out of the pit a dozen times in the two races. But I didn't jump at conclusions simply because the doctor examined her heart six or seven times a day. I knew he could never locate her trouble with a stethoscope.

'Lean over here, Robert,' Mrs Layden said. It was the first time she had ever used my given name and I was a little embarrassed. I leaned over the railing, swaying my body so nobody could say I was violating the rules of the contest by not being in motion. The hall was packed and jammed. 'You know I'm your friend, don't you?' Mrs Layden said.

'Yes'm, I know that,'

'You know I got you your sponsor, don't you?'

'Yes'm, I know that.'

'You trust me, don't you?'

'Yes'm, I trust you.'

'Robert – Gloria's not the right kind of girl for you.'

I didn't say anything, wondering what was coming next. I had never been able to understand why Mrs Layden had taken such an interest in me unless. . . . But it couldn't be that. She was old enough to be my grandmother.

'She'll never be any good,' Mrs Layden said. 'She's an evil person and she'll wreck your life. You don't want your life wrecked, do you?'

'She's not going to wreck my life,' I said.

'Promise me when you get out of this you'll never see her again.'

'Oh, I'm not going to marry her or anything like that,' I said. 'I'm not in love with her. She's all right. She just gets a little depressed sometimes.'

'She's not depressed,' Mrs Layden said. 'She's bitter. She hates everything and everybody. She's cruel and she's dangerous.'

'I didn't know you felt that way about her, Mrs Layden.'

'I'm an old woman,' she said. 'I'm a very, very – old, old woman. I know what I'm talking about. When this thing is over – Robert,' she said suddenly. 'I'm not as poor as you think I am. I look poor but I'm not poor at all. I'm rich. I'm very rich. I'm very eccentric. When you get out of here – '

'Hello – ' Gloria said, coming from nowhere.

' – Hello,' Mrs Layden said.

'What's the matter?' Gloria asked quickly. 'Am I interrupting something?'

'You're not interrupting anything,' I told her.

Mrs Layden opened the newspaper and started reading it. Gloria and I walked towards the platform.

'What was she saying about me?' Gloria asked.

'Nothing,' I said. 'We were just talking about the marathon closing – '

'You were talking about something else too. Why did she shut up like a clam when I got there?'

'You're imagining things – ' I said.

'Ladies and gentlemen – ' Rocky said into the microphone, ' – or maybe after reading the newspapers,' he went on when the crowd had quieted down, 'I should say – Fellow Morons.' There was a big laugh at this; the crowd knew what he meant. 'You can see we're still going in the world's championship marathon dance,' he said, 'and we'll keep on going until only one contestant is left – the final winner. I want to thank you very much for coming out tonight and I'd like to remind you that tomorrow night is the night you can't afford to miss, our big public wedding, when Couple No. 71 – Vee Lovell and Mary Hawley – will be married right here before your very eyes by a well-known minister of the city. If you haven't made your reservations you better do so at once.

'And now, before the derby starts, I'd like to introduce a few of our celebrities – ' He looked at a piece of paper. 'Ladies and gentlemen, one of our honour guests is none other than that handsome screen star, Bill Boyd. Will you take a bow, Mr Boyd? – '

Bill (Screen) Boyd stood up, taking a bow, while the audience applauded.

'Next, another screen and stage star – Ken Murray. Mr Murray has a party of distinguished guests with him. I wonder if he'd come up to the platform and introduce them himself? – '

The audience applauded loudly. Murray hesitated, but finally stepped over the railing and went to the platform.

'All right folks – ' he said, taking the microphone. 'First a young featured player, Miss Anita Louise – '

Miss Louise stood.

' – and now Miss June Clyde – '

Miss Clyde stood.

' – Miss Sue Carol – '

Miss Carol stood.

' – Tom Brown – '

Tom Brown stood.

' – Thornton Freeland – '

Thornton Freeland stood.

' – and that's all, folks – '

Murray shook hands with Rocky and went back to his party.

'Ladies and gentlemen – ' Rocky said.

'There's a big director over there he didn't introduce,' I said to Gloria. 'There's Frank Borzage. Let's go speak to him – '

'For what?' Gloria said.

'He's a director, isn't he? He might help you get in pictures – '

'The hell with pictures,' Gloria said 'I wish I was dead – '

'I'm going,' I said.

I strolled down the floor in front of the boxes, feeling very self-conscious. Two or three times I almost lost my nerve and turned back.

'It's worth it,' I told myself. 'He's one of the finest directors in the world. Some day I'll be as famous as he is and then I'll remind him of this – '

'Hello, Mr Borzage,' I said.

'Hello, son,' he said. 'Are you going to win tonight?'

'I hope so . . . I saw "No Greater Glory". I thought it was swell,' I said.

'I'm glad you liked it – '

'That's what I want to be some day,' I said. 'A director like you – '

'I hope you are,' he said.

'Well – ' I said, 'good-bye – '

I went back to the platform.

'That was Frank Borzage,' I said to Kid Kamm.

'Yeah? – '

'He's a big director,' I explained.

'Oh – ' the Kid said.

'All right – ' Rocky said. 'Are the judges ready? Have they got their score sheets, Rollo? – All right, kids – '

We moved out to the starting line.

'Let's not take any chances tonight,' I whispered to Gloria. 'We can't fool around – '

'On your marks, there, kids,' Rocky said. 'Stand by nurses and trainers – Hold your hats, ladies and gentlemen – Orchestra, get ready to give – '

He shot the pistol himself.

Gloria and I jumped away, pushing through into second place, directly behind Kid Kamm and Jackie Miller. They were in front, the position usually held by James and Ruby Bates. As I went into the first turn I thought about James and Ruby, wondering where they were. It didn't seem like a derby without them.

At the finish of the first lap Mack Aston and Bess Cartwright sprinted in front of us and went into second place. I began to heel-and-toe faster than I ever had before. I knew I had to. All the weaklings had been eliminated. All these couples were fast.

I stayed in third place for six or seven laps and the audience began howling and yelling for us to move up. I was afraid to try that. You can pass a fast team only on the turn and that takes a lot of energy. So far Gloria was holding up fine and I didn't want to put too much pressure on her. I wasn't worried as long as she could keep propelling herself.

After eight minutes I commenced to get hot. I yanked off my sweatshirt and tossed it to a trainer. Gloria did likewise. Most of the girls were out of their sweatshirts now and the audience was howling. When the girls removed their sweatshirts they wore only small brassieres, and as they trotted around the track their breasts bounced up and down.

'Everything is fine now unless somebody challenges us,' I told myself.

Just then we were challenged. Pedro Ortega and Lillian Bacon sped up alongside, trying to get inside at the turn. This was about the only way to pass a couple but it was not as easy as it sounds. You had to get at least two paces ahead on the straightaway and then swing sharply over at the turn. This was what Pedro had in the back of his mind. They collided with us at the turn, but Gloria managed to keep her feet and I dragged her through, holding our place.

I heard the audience gasp and I knew that meant somebody was staggering. In a moment I heard a body hit the floor. I didn't look around; I kept pounding. This was old stuff to me now. When I got on the straightaway and could look without breaking my stride, I saw it was Mary Hawley, Vee Lovell's partner, who was in the pit. The nurses and trainers were working on her and the doctor was using his stethoscope –

'Give the solo the inside, kids – ' Rocky yelled.

I moved over and Vee passed me. Now he had to make two laps to our one. He glanced in the pit as he passed, a look of agony on his face. I knew he was not in pain; he was only wondering when his partner would be out. . . . On his fourth solo lap she got up, coupling on again.

I signalled to the nurse for a wet towel and on the next lap she slammed it around my neck. I stuck the end of it between my teeth.

'Four minutes to go – ' Rocky yelled.

This was one of the closest derbies we'd ever had. The Kid and Jackie were setting a terrific pace. I knew Gloria and I were in no danger as long as we held our own but you never could tell when your partner would collapse. Past a certain point you kept moving automatically, without actually being conscious of moving. One moment you would be travelling at top speed and the next moment you started falling. This was what I was afraid of with Gloria – collapsing. She was beginning to drag on my belt a little.

'Keep going!' I shouted to her in my mind, slowing down a fraction, hoping to relieve the strain on her. Pedro and Lillian evidently had been waiting for this. They shot by us on the turn, taking third place. Directly behind me I could hear the pounding of the others and I realized the entire field was bunched at Gloria's heels. I had absolutely no margin now.

I hitched my hip up high. That was a signal for Gloria to shift her hold on the belt. She did, changing to the right hand.

'Thank God,' I said to myself. That was a good sign. That proved she was thinking all right.

'One minute to go – ' Rocky announced.

I put on the steam now. Kid Kamm and Jackie had slowed the pace somewhat, thus slowing Mack and Bess and Pedro and Lillian. Gloria and I were between them and the others. It was a bad position. I prayed that nobody behind us had the energy for a spurt because I realized that the slightest bump would break Gloria's stride and put her on the floor. And if anybody hit the floor now. . . .

I used every ounce of my strength to move up, to get just one step ahead, to remove that threat from behind. . . . When the gun sounded for the finish I turned around to catch Gloria. But she didn't faint. She staggered into my arms, shiny with perspiration, fighting to get air.

'Want a nurse?' Rocky yelled from the platform.

'She's all right,' I said. 'Let her rest a minute – '

Most of the girls were being helped into the dressing room, but the boys crowded around the platform to see who had been disqualified. The judges had handed their tally sheets to Rollo and Rocky, who were checking them.

'Ladies and gentlemen – ' Rocky announced in a minute or two. 'Here are the results of the most sensational derby you have ever seen. First place – Couple No. 18, Kid Kamm and Jackie Miller. Second place – Mack Aston and Bess Cartwright. Third place – Pedro Ortega and Lillian Bacon. Fourth place – Robert Syverten and Gloria Beatty. Those were the winners – and now, the losers – the last team to finish – the couple that, under the rules and regulations, is disqualified and out of the marathon dance. That is Couple No. 11 – Jere Flint and Vera Rosenfield – '

'You're crazy!' Jere Flint shouted, loud enough for everybody in the hall to hear. 'That's wrong – ' he said, moving closer to the platform.

'Look at 'em yourself,' Rocky said, handing him the tally sheets.

'I wish it had been us,' Gloria said, lifting her head. 'I wish I had thrown the race – '

'Sh-h-h – ' I said.

'I don't give a damn what these score cards say; they're wrong,' Jere Flint said, handing them back to Rocky. 'I know they're wrong. How the hell could we get eliminated when we weren't last?'

'Are you able to keep track of the laps while you're racing?' Rocky asked. He was trying to show Jere up. He knew it wasn't possible for anybody to do that.

'I can't do that,' Jere said. 'But I know we didn't go into the pit and Mary did. We started ahead of Vee and Mary and we finished ahead of 'em – '

'How about that, mister?' Rocky said to a man standing near-by. 'You checked Couple No. 11 – '

'You're mistaken, fellow,' the man said to Jere. 'I checked you carefully – '

'It's too bad, son,' Socks Donald said, coming through the crowd of judges. 'You had tough luck – '

'It wasn't tough luck; it was a goddam frameup,' Jere said. 'You ain't kidding anybody. If Vee and Mary had been eliminated you wouldn't have a wedding tomorrow – '

'Now – now – ' Socks said. 'You run on to the dressing room – '

'Okay,' Jere said. He walked over to the man who had kept check on him and Vera. 'How much is Socks giving you for this?' he asked.

'I don't know what you're talking about – '

Jere turned sidewise, slamming the man in the mouth with his fist, knocking him down.

Socks ran over to Jere, squaring off, glaring at him, his hand in his hip pocket.

'If you pull that blackjack on me I'll make you eat it,' Jere told him. Then he walked away, going across the floor towards the dressing room.

The audience was standing, jabbering, trying to see what was going on.

'Let's get dressed,' I said to Gloria.

. . . upon the
19th day of
the month
of September,
in the year
of our Lord,
1935 . . .

...*chapter twelve*

HOURS ELAPSED   879
Couples Remaining 20

All day Gloria had been very morbid. I asked her a hundred times what she was thinking about. 'Nothing,' she would reply. *I realize now how stupid I was. I should have known what she was thinking. Now that I look back on that night I don't see how I possibly could have been so stupid. But in those days I was dumb about a lot of things . . . The judge is sitting up there, making his speech, looking through his glasses at me, but his words are doing the same thing to my body that his eyesight is doing to his glasses – going right through without stopping, rushing out of the way of each succeeding look and each succeeding word. I am not hearing the judge with my ears and my brain any more than the lenses of his glass are catching and imprisoning each look that comes through them. I hear him with my feet and my legs and torso and arms, with everything but my ears and brain. With my ears and brain I hear a newsboy in the street shouting something about King Alexander, I hear the rolling of the street cars, I hear automobiles, I hear the warning bells of the traffic semaphores; in the courtroom I hear people breathing and moving their feet, I hear the wood squeaking in a bench, I hear the light splash as someone spits in the cuspidor. All these things I hear with my ears and my brain, but I hear the judge with my body only. If you ever hear a judge say to you what this one is saying to me, you will know what I mean.*

This was one day Gloria had no reason to be morbid. The crowds had been coming and going all day, since noon the place had been packed, and now, just before the wedding, there were very few vacant seats left and most of them had been reserved. The entire hall had been decorated with so many flags and so much red, white and blue bunting that you expected any moment to hear firecrackers go off and the band play the national anthem. The whole day had been full of excitement: the workmen decorating the interior, the big crowds, the rehearsals for the wedding, the rumours that the Morals League women were coming down to set fire to the hall – and the two complete new outfits the Jonathan Beer people had sent Gloria and me.

This was one day Gloria had no reason to be morbid, but she was more morbid than ever.

'Son – ' a man called from a box. I had never seen him before. He was motioning for me to come over.

'You won't be in that seat long,' I told him in my mind. 'That's Mrs Layden's regular seat. When she comes you'll have to move.'

'Aren't you the boy of Couple 22?' he asked.

'Yessir,' I said.

'Where's your partner?'

'She's down there – ' I replied, pointing towards the platform where Gloria stood with the other girls.

'Get her,' the man said. 'I want to meet her.'

'All right,' I said, going to get Gloria. 'Now who can that be?' I asked myself.

'There's a man down here who wants to meet you,' I said to Gloria.

'I don't want to meet anybody.'

'This man's no bum,' I said. 'He's well-dressed. He looks like somebody.'

'I don't care what he looks like,' she said.

'He may be a producer, 'I said. 'Maybe you've made a hit with him. Maybe this is your break.'

'The hell with my break,' she said.

'Come on,' I said. 'The man's waiting.'

She finally came with me.

'This motion picture business is a lousy business,' she said. 'You have to meet people you don't want to meet and you have to be nice to people whose guts you hate. I'm glad I'm through with it.'

'You're just starting with it,' I said, trying to cheer her up. *I never paid any attention to her remark then, but now I realize it was the most significant thing she had ever said.*

'Here she is – ' I said to the man.

'You don't know who I am, do you?' the man asked.

'No, sir – '

'My name is Maxwell,' he said. 'I'm the advertising manager for Jonathan Beer.'

'How do you do, Mr Maxwell,' I said, reaching over to shake hands with him. 'This is my partner, Gloria Beatty. I want to thank you for sponsoring us.'

'Don't thank me,' he said. 'Thank Mrs Layden. She brought you to my attention. Did you get your packages today?'

'Yessir,' I said, 'and they came just in time. We certainly needed clothes. These marathon dances are pretty hard on your clothes. Have you ever been here before?'

'No, and I wouldn't be here now if Mrs Layden hadn't insisted. She's been telling me about the derbies. Are you having one tonight?'

'A little thing like a wedding couldn't stop the derby,' I said. 'It goes on right after the ceremony – '

'So long – ' Gloria said, walking off.

'Did I say something wrong?' Mr Maxwell asked.

'No, sir – she's got to go down there and get her final instructions. The wedding starts pretty soon.'

He frowned and I could tell he knew I was merely lying to cover Gloria's bad manners. He watched Gloria walking down the floor a minute and then looked back at me. 'What chance do you have to win the derby tonight?' he asked.

'We've got a good chance,' I said. 'Of course, the big thing is not so much to win as it is to keep from losing. If you finish last you're disqualified.'

'Suppose Jonathan Beer offered twenty-five dollars to the winner,' he said. 'You think you'd have a chance to get it?'

'We'll certainly try like the devil,' I told him.

'In that case – all right,' he said, looking me up and down. 'Mrs Layden tells me you're ambitious to get in the movies?'

'I am,' I said. 'Not as an actor though, I want to be a director.'

'You wouldn't like a job in the brewery business, eh?'

'I don't believe I would – '

'Have you ever directed a picture?'

'No, sir, but I'm not afraid to try it. I know I could make good,' I said. 'Oh, I don't mean a big feature like Boleslawsky or Mamoulian or King Vidor would make – I mean something else at first – '

'For instance – '

'Well, like a two – or three-reel short. What a junkman does all day, or the life of an ordinary man – you know, who makes thirty dollars a week and has to raise kids and buy a home and a car and a radio – the kind of a guy bill collectors are always after. Something different, with camera angles to help tell the story – '

'I see – ' he said.

'I didn't mean to bore you,' I said, 'but it's so seldom I can find anybody who'll listen to me that when I do I never know when to stop talking.'

'I'm not bored. As a matter of fact, I'm very much interested,' he said. 'But maybe I've said too much myself – '

'Good evening – ' Mrs Layden said, entering the box. Mr Maxwell stood up. 'That's my seat, John,' Mrs Layden said. 'You sit over here.' Mr Maxwell laughed and took another chair. 'My, my, don't you look handsome,' Mrs Layden said to me.

'This is the first time in my life I ever had on a tuxedo,' I said blushing. 'Mr Donald rented tuxedos for all the boys and dresses for the girls. We're all in the wedding march.'

'What do you think of him, John?' Mrs Layden asked Mr Maxwell.

'He's all right,' Mr Maxwell said.

'I trust John's judgement implicitly,' Mrs Layden said to me. I began to understand now why Mr Maxwell had asked me all those questions.

' – Down this way, you kids – ' Rocky said into the microphone. 'Down this way – Ladies and gentlemen. We are about to have the public wedding between Couple No. 71 – Vee Lovell and Mary Hawley – and please remember, the entertainment for the night is not over when the marriage is finished. That's only the beginnin' – ' he said; ' – only the beginnin'. After the wedding we have the derby – '

He leaned over while Socks Donald whispered something to him.

'Ladies and gentlemen,' Rocky announced. 'I take great pleasure in introducing the minister who will perform the service – a minister you all know, Rev. Oscar Gilder. Will you come up, Mr Gilder?'

The minister came out on the floor and walked towards the platfomm while the audience applauded.

'Get your places,' Socks said to us. We went to our assigned positions, the girls on one side of the platform and the boys on the other.

'Before the grand march starts,' Rocky said, 'I want to thank those who have made this feature possible.' He looked at a sheet of paper. 'The bride's wedding gown,' he said, 'was donated by Mr Samuels of the Bon-Top Shop. Will you stand, Mr Samuels?'

Mr Samuels stood, bowing to the applause.

'Her shoes were donated by the Main Street Slipper Shop – Is Mr Davis here? Stand up, Mr Davis.'

Mr Davis stood.

' – Her stockings and silken – er – you-know-whats were donated by the Polly-Darling Girls' Bazaar. Mr Lightfoot, where are you? – '

Mr Lightfoot stood as the audience howled.

' – and her hair was marcelled by the Pompadour Beauty Shop. Is Miss Smith here?'

Miss Smith stood.

' – And the groom's outfit, from head to foot, was donated by the Tower Outfitting Company. Mr Tower – '

'All the flowers in the hall and that the girls are wearing are the gift of the Sycamore Ridge Nursery. Mr Dupré – '

Mr Dupré stood.

' – And now, ladies and gentlemen, I turn the microphone over to the Rev. Oscar Gilder, who will perform the ceremony for these marvellous kids – '

He handed the microphone stand to Rollo, who stood it on the floor in front of the platform. Rev. Gilder moved behind it, nodding to the orchestra, and the wedding march began.

The procession started, the boys on one side and the girls on the other, going down to the end of the hall and then back to the minister. It was the first time I had seen some of the girls when they weren't in slacks or track suits.

We had rehearsed the march twice that afternoon, being taught to come to a full stop after each step before taking another. When the bride and groom came into view from behind the platform, the audience cheered and applauded.

Mrs Layden nodded to me as I passed.

At the platform we took our places while Vee and Mary, and Kid Kamm and Jackie Miller, the best man and the maid-of-honour, continued to where the minister was standing. He motioned for the orchestra to stop and began the ceremony. All during the ceremony I kept looking at Gloria. I hadn't a chance to tell her how rude she had been to Mr Maxwell, so I tried to catch her eye to let her know I had plenty to tell her when we got together.

' – And I now pronounce you man and wife – ' Dr Gilder said. He bowed his head and began to pray:

The Lord is my shepherd; I shall not want. He maketh me lie down in green pastures: He leadeth me beside the still waters. He restoreth my soul: He leadeth me in the paths of righteousness for His name's sake. Yea, though I walk through the valley of the shadow of death, I will fear no evil: for thou art with me; thy rod and thy staff they comfort me. Thou preparest a table before me in the presence of mine enemies: thou anointest my head with oil; my cup runneth over. Surely goodness and mercy shall follow me all the days of my life; and I will dwell in the house of the Lord for ever.

. . . When the minister had finished Vee kissed Mary timidly on the cheek and we swarmed around. The hall rocked with applause and shouts.

'Just a minute – just a minute – ' Rocky yelled into the microphone. 'Just a minute, ladies and gentlemen – '

The confusion died down and at that moment, at the opposite end of the hall, in the Palm Garden, there was the clear, distinct sound of glass shattering.

'Don't – ' a man screamed. Five shots followed this, so close together they sounded like one solid strip of noise.

Instantly the audience roared.

'Keep your seats – keep your seats – ' Rocky yelled. . . .

The other boys and girls were running towards the Palm Garden to see what had happened, and I joined them. Socks Donald passed me, reaching into his hip pocket.

I jumped over the railing into an empty box and followed Socks into the Palm Garden. A crowd of people were standing in a circle, looking down and jabbering at each other. Socks pushed through and I followed him.

A man was dead on the floor.

'Who did it?' Socks asked.

'A guy over there – ' somebody said.

Socks pushed out with me behind him. I was a little surprised to discover Gloria was directly behind me.

The man who had done the shooting was standing at the bar, leaning on his elbow. Blood was streaming down his face. Socks went up to him.

'He started it, Socks,' the man said. ' – He was trying to kill me with a beer bottle – '

'Monk, you son of a bitch – ' Socks said, hitting him in the face with the blackjack. Monk sagged against the bar but did not fall. Socks continued to hit him in the face with

111

the blackjack, again and again and again, splattering blood
all over everything and everybody nearby. He literally beat
the man to the floor.

'Hey, Socks – ' somebody called.

Thirty feet away there was another group of people
standing in a circle, looking down and jabbering to each
other. We pushed our way through – and there she lay.

'Goddam – ' Socks Donald said.

It was Mrs Layden, a single hole in the front of her
forehead. John Maxwell was kneeling beside her, holding
her head . . . then he placed the head gently on the floor,
and stood up. Mrs Layden's head slowly turned sidewise and
a little pool of blood that had collected in the crater of her
eye spilled out on the floor.

John Maxwell saw Gloria and me.

'She was coming around to be a judge in the derby,' he
said. 'She was hit by a stray bullet – '

'I wish it was me – ' Gloria said under her breath.

'Goddam – ' Socks Donald said.

We were all assembled in the girls' dressing room. There
were very few people outside in the hall, only the police and
several reporters.

'I guess you kids know why I got you in here,' Socks said
slowly, 'and I guess you know what I'm going to say. There
ain't no use for anybody to feel bad about what's happened
– it's just one of those things. It's tough on you kids and it's
tough on me. We had just got the marathon started good –

'Rocky and I have been talking it over and we've decided

to take the thousand-dollar prize and split it up between all of you – and I'm going to throw in another grand myself. That'll give everybody fifty bucks apiece. Is that fair?'

'Yes – ' we said.

'Don't you think there's any chance to keep going?' Kid Kamm asked.

'Not a chance,' Socks said, shaking his head. Not with that Purity League after us – '

'Kids,' Rocky said, 'we've had a lot of fun and I've enjoyed working with you. Maybe some time we can have another marathon dance – '

'When do we get this dough?' Vee Lovell asked.

'In the morning,' Socks said. 'Any of you kids that want to can stay here tonight, just like you been doing. But if you want to leave, there's nothing to stop you. I'll have the dough for you in the morning any time after ten. Now, I'll say so-long – I got to go to police headquarters.'

. . . in the manner provided by the laws of the State of California. And . . .

...*chapter thirteen*

Gloria and I walked across the dance floor, my heels making so much noise I couldn't be sure they belonged to me. Rocky was standing at the front door with a policeman.

'Where you kids going?' Rocky asked.

'To get some air,' Gloria said.

'Coming back?'

'We'll be back,' I told him. 'We're just going to get a little air. It's been a long time since we been outside – '

'Don't be long,' Rocky said, looking at Gloria and wetting his lips significantly.

'—you,' Gloria said, going outside.

It was after two o'clock in the morning. The air was damp and thick and clean. It was so thick and so clean I could feel my lungs biting it off in huge chunks.

'I bet you are glad to get that kind of air,' I said to my lungs.

I turned around and looked at the building.

'So that's where we've been all the time,' I said. 'Now I know how Jonah felt when he looked at the whale.'

'Come on,' Gloria said.

We walked around the side of the building on to the pier.

It stretched out over the ocean as far as I could see, rising and falling and groaning and creaking with the movements of the water.

'It's a wonder the waves don't wash this pier away,' I said.

'You're hipped on the subject of waves,' Gloria said.

'No, I'm not,' I said.

'That's all you've been talking about for a month – '

'All right, stand still a minute and you'll see what I mean. You can feel it rising and falling – '

'I can feel it without standing still,' she said, 'but that's no reason to get yourself in a sweat. It's been going on for a million years.'

'Don't think I'm crazy about this ocean,' I said. 'It'll be all right with me if I never see it again. I've had enough ocean to last me the rest of my life.'

We sat down on a bench that was wet with spray. Up towards the end of the pier several men were fishing over the railing. The night was black; there was no moon, no stars. An irregular line of white foam marked the shore.

'This air is fine,' I said.

Gloria said nothing staring into the distance. Far down the shore on a point there were lights.

'That's Malibu,' I said. 'Where all the movie stars live.'

'What are you going to do now?' she finally said.

'I don't know exactly. I thought I'd go see Mr Maxwell tomorrow. Maybe I could get him to do something. He certainly seemed interested.'

'Always tomorrow,' she said. 'The big break is always coming tomorrow.'

Two men passed by, carrying deep-sea fishing poles. One of them was dragging a four-foot hammerhead shark behind him.

'This baby'll never do any more damage,' he said to the other man. . . .

'What are you going to do?' I asked Gloria.

'I'm going to get off this merry-go-round,' she said. 'I'm through with the whole stinking thing.'

'What thing?'

'Life,' she said.

'Why don't you try to help yourself?' I said. 'You got the wrong attitude about everything.'

'Don't lecture to me,' she said.

'I'm not lecturing,' I said, 'but you ought to change your attitude. On the level. It affects everybody you come in contact with. Take me, for example. Before I met you I didn't see how I could miss succeeding. I never even thought of failing. And now – '

'Who taught you that speech?' she asked. 'You never thought that up by yourself.'

'Yes, I did,' I said.

She looked down the ocean towards Malibu. 'Oh, what's the use in me kidding myself – ' she said in a moment. 'I know where I stand . . .'

I did not say anything, looking at the ocean and thinking about Hollywood, wondering if I'd ever been there or was I going to wake up in a minute back in Arkansas and have to hurry down and get my newspapers before it got daylight.

' – Sonofabitch,' Gloria was saying to herself. 'You

needn't look at me that way,' she said, 'I know I'm no good – '

'She's right,' I said to myself; 'she's exactly right. She's no good – '

'I wish I'd died that time in Dallas,' she said. 'I always will think that doctor saved my life for just one reason – '

I did not say anything to that, still looking at the ocean and thinking how exactly right she was about being no good and that it was too bad she didn't die that time in Dallas. She certainly would have been better off dead.

'I'm just a misfit. I haven't got anything to give anybody,' she was saying. 'Stop looking at me that way,' she said.

'I'm not looking at you any way,' I said. 'You can't see my face – '

'Yes, I can,' she said.

She was lying. She couldn't see my face. It was too dark.

'Don't you think we ought to go inside?' I said. 'Rocky wanted to see you – '

'That—,' she said. 'I know what he wants, but he'll never get it again. Nobody else will, either.'

'What?' I said.

'Don't you know?'

'Don't I know what.' I said.

'What Rocky wants.'

'Oh – ' I said. 'Sure. It just dawned on me.'

'That's all any man wants,' she said, 'but that's all right. Oh, I didn't mind giving it to Rocky; he was doing me as much of a favour as I did him – but suppose I get caught?'

'You're not just thinking of that, are you?' I asked.

'Yes, I am. Always before this time I was able to take care of myself. Suppose I do have a kid?' she said. 'You know what it'll grow up to be, don't you. Just like us.'

'I don't want that,' she said. 'Anyway, I'm finished. I think it's a lousy world and I'm finished. I'd be better off dead and so would everybody else. I ruin everything I get around. You said so yourself.'

'When did I say anything like that?'

'A few minutes ago. You said before you met me you never even thought of failing. . . . Well, it isn't my fault. I can't help it. I tried to kill myself once, but I didn't and I've never had the nerve to try again. . . . You want to do the world a favour? . . .' she asked.

I did not say anything, listening to the ocean slosh against the pilings, feeling the pier rise and fall, and thinking that she was right about everything she had said.

Gloria was fumbling in her purse. When her hand came out it was holding a small pistol. I had never seen the pistol before, but I was not surprised. I was not in the least surprised.

'Here – ' she said, offering it to me.

'I don't want it. Put it away,' I said. 'Come on, let's go back inside. I'm cold – '

'Take it and pinch-hit for God,' she said, pressing it into my hand. 'Shoot me. It's the only way to get me out of my misery.'

119

'She's right,' I said to myself. 'It's the only way to get her out of her misery.' *When I was a little kid I used to spend the summers on my grandfather's farm in Arkansas. One day I was standing by the smokehouse watching my grandmother making lye soap in a big iron kettle when my grandfather came across the yard, very excited. 'Nellie broke her leg,' my grandfather said. My grandmother and I went over the stile into the garden where my grandfather had been ploughing. Old Nellie was on the ground whimpering, still hitched to the plough. We stood there looking at her, just looking at her. My grandfather came back with the gun he had carried at Chickamauga Ridge. 'She stepped in a hole,' he said, patting Nellie's head. My grandmother turned me around, facing the other way. I started crying. I heard a shot. I still hear that shot. I ran over and fell down on the ground, hugging her neck. I loved that horse. I hated my grandfather. I got up and went to him, beating his legs with my fists. . . . Later that day he explained that he loved Nellie too, but that he had to shoot her. 'It was the kindest thing to do,' he said. 'She was no more good. It was the only way to get her out of her misery. . . .'*

I had the pistol in my hand.

'All right,' I said to Gloria. 'Say when.'

'I'm ready.'

'Where? – '

'Right here. In the side of my head.'

The pier jumped as a big wave broke.

'Now? – '

'Now.'

I shot her.

The pier moved again, and the water made a sucking noise as it slipped back into the ocean.

I threw the pistol over the railing.

One policeman sat in the rear with me while the other one drove. We were travelling very fast and the siren was blowing. It was the same kind of a siren they had used at the marathon dance when they wanted to wake us up.

'Why did you kill her?' the policeman in the rear seat asked.

'She asked me to,' I said.

'You hear that, Ben?'

'Ain't he an obliging bastard?' Ben said, over his shoulder.

'Is that the only reason you got?' the policeman in the rear seat asked.

'They shoot horses, don't they?' I said.

. . . may God
have mercy
on your
soul . . .

Horace McCoy

by William Marling

Professor of English,
Case Western Reserve University

Horace McCoy (1897–1955) was born to a poor but literate Irish-American family in or near Nashville, Tennessee. He once described his parents as 'book rich and money poor'.[1] Quitting school at sixteen, he worked as a cab-driver, mechanic and travelling salesman, then joined the Air National Guard and got himself sent to France to serve as bombardier on De Havilland bombers. On August 5, 1918, when his pilot was killed, McCoy took over the controls, shot down an enemy plane and flew his own home, despite twice being wounded by machine-gun fire. After recovery he was given the Croix de Guerre. By November he was piloting his own fighter, but the war ended before he could 'outshine [Eddie] Rickenbacker', as he promised his parents in a letter.[2] Nevertheless, he logged four-hundred hours over enemy territory, was wounded again and pinned with another medal.

Like detective novelist Raoul Whitfield, who also served as an aviator during World War I, McCoy aspired to be a writer, but he knew he needed to learn the trade. He found a job with one Dallas paper as a sports/crime reporter, then moved up to its rival as sports editor. He used his position to run with the rich, to drive big cars and to dress like a dandy. 'Mack was consumed with ambition,' said a friend, 'he always had big ideas.'[3] McCoy married and had a son, but he abandoned his family for the Dallas society scene – an accomplished swimmer, golfer and tennis player, he fit right in. He began to publish short stories in *Detective-Dragnet* and *Detective Action*, and also to act with the Dallas Little Theatre in 1925, for which he won national attention.

By 1927, however, his habits outpaced his means and he needed more income. He sent a tale of South Seas island-hopping to *Black Mask* magazine, whose readers had an insatiable hunger for air-adventure fiction. The celebrated editor 'Cap' Shaw, who purchased it, urged McCoy on to more air fiction. Not as prolific as other *Black Mask* writers, McCoy nevertheless created one of its strongest serial heroes. Captain Jerry Frost was a Texas Ranger who flew small aircraft with the Air Border Patrol. Romantic and often over-written, the Frost tales sprouted declarations about life and death like crabgrass, despite Shaw's editing. In 1929, probably because of his debts and social excesses, McCoy had to leave his Dallas newspaper job. He edited a local magazine, *Dallasine*, but it shut down on the cusp of the Great Depression. He then eloped with a debutante, but her parents had the marriage annulled, and McCoy woke up in a run-down boarding-house of bohemians and failed artists, where he began to churn out pulp fiction for six or seven magazines just to stay alive. Still passionate about flying, McCoy often borrowed planes from former social acquaintances. One of these he crashed while trying to set a local altitude record.

An MGM scout who had seen his theatre work set up a screen test, so McCoy went to Hollywood. But the screen test failed and the Great Depression deepened. A tramp, a bum, McCoy slept in abandoned cars, picked fruit and vegetables in the Imperial Valley, worked as a soda jerk, a bodyguard and a picket – until he was hired as a bouncer at a marathon dance contest in Santa Monica. Still focused on a Hollywood career, he wrote up this experience as a movie script called *Marathon Dancers*. It did not sell, but he got taken on as a contract writer with RKO studios, beginning what he called 'my notable career as a studio hack'.[4] He married again, once more to the ire of the bride's parents, who left her penniless. But McCoy managed to finish a novel based on his movie script, which was titled *They Shoot Horses, Don't They?* and published in 1935. Although later a favourite of French existentialists, McCoy's book sold only 3,000 copies the first year. It tells the story of failed actress Gloria, who in desperation enters a marathon dance contest that becomes an endurance nightmare. Realising that this punishment *is* her life, Gloria convinces her partner to kill her -- a testament to the meaning/meaninglessness of life. By turns lyric and grim, the novel combines irony and fear with a subtlety and rawness that would mark the peak of McCoy's writing career.

But McCoy thought that he was above the pulps now. He stopped writing for *Black Mask*, and even complained about the B movies he worked on: 'These bastards never give me a shot at the A pics,' he said. But he stayed with the studios and wrote two more books, *No Pockets in a Shroud* (1937) and *I Should Have Stayed Home* (1938). Both were autobiographical and bitter about his Hollywood experiences.

Finally resigning himself to Hollywood, McCoy turned out sixteen original scripts between 1937 and 1940. In

1942 he wrote a major movie, *Gentleman Jim*, for Errol Flynn. In the mid-1940s French writers such as Jean-Paul Sartre, André Gide and André Malraux discovered *They Shoot Horses, Don't They?* and Simone de Beauvoir said that it 'was the first existentialist novel to have appeared in America'. Europeans began to rank him beside Faulkner, Steinbeck and Hemingway. McCoy, however, was broke, depressed and 'fat from too much food and booze'.[5] What inspired him for a last big effort was a manuscript he had been working on, *Kiss Tomorrow Goodbye*, which Random House liked and published in 1948. His best work since *They Shoot Horses, Don't They?*, the novel displayed a masterly alternation between action and reflection. East Coast reviewers may not have liked it, but Warner Brothers bought the story as a vehicle for James Cagney, who wanted another 'really nasty role' to cement his screen persona after portraying a psychotic criminal in *White Heat* (1949). On top of this, in early 1951, McCoy sold an original script called *Scalpel* to Hall Wallis Productions for $100,000. Both the novel and the movie were winners, and McCoy was working on a new book called *The Hard Rock Man* when a heart attack felled him. At fifty-eight, McCoy died broke on December 15, 1955, and his widow had to sell his books and jazz collection to pay for his funeral.[6]

1. John Thomas Stuark, *The Life and Writings of Horace McCoy*. Berkeley: University of California, 1976, 21.
2. McCoy in William Nolan, *The Black Mask Boys*. New York: William Morrow, 1985, 177–78.

3.   McCoy's friend in Nolan, *Black Mask*, 178.

4.   McCoy in Nolan, *Black Mask*, 180–81.

5.   de Beauvoir and McCoy in Nolan, 182.

6.   Nolan, 184.

Other Serpent's Tail titles of interest

Boy A
Jonathan Trigell

'Creepy and involving . . . From the beginning, Trigell weaves a sense of drama and a disturbing feeling of inevitability' *Independent*

'Trigell brilliantly depicts the pressures of living with a terrible secret . . . written with a naive clarity which evokes the unfamiliar wonders of the outside world' *Guardian*

'A fine and moving debut novel . . . Harrowing at times, this compulsively readable novel is more optimistic than it sounds . . . a rare treat' *Independent*

'Eerie parallels to the Bulger case abound in this modern day immorality tale about the attempted rehabilitation of a child implicated in murder . . . delivered with a horrific sense of foreboding' *Arena*

'A shocker of a first novel . . . told with extraordinary restraint' *New York Times*

Boy A is a 2007 film directed by John Crowley, with screenplay by Mark O'Rowe. Starring Andrew Garfield and Peter Mullan, it won 4 BAFTA awards, including best actor for Andrew Garfield and best director for John Crowley. Available on DVD from all good retailers & online.

Red Riding
David Peace

'British crime fiction's most exciting new voice in decades'
GQ

'Quite simply, this is the future of British crime fiction'
Time Out

'The pace is relentless, the style staccato-plus and the morality bleak and forlorn . . . Peace's voice is powerful and unique' *Guardian*

'Breathless, extravagant, ultra-violent' *Independent on Sunday*

Red Riding Trilogy is a 2009 film directed by Anand Tucker and Julian Jarrold, starring Rebecca Hall and Brendan McCoy. Available on DVD from all good retailers & online.

The Piano Teacher
Elfriede Jelinek

'In this demented love story the hunter is the hunted, pain is pleasure, and spite and self-contempt seep from every pore' *Guardian*

'A dazzling performance that will make the blood run cold' Walter Abish

'A brilliant, deadly book' Elizabeth Young

'Some may find Ms Jelinek's ruthlessly unsentimental approach – not to mention her image of Vienna as a bleak city of porno shops, poor immigrants and loveless copulations – too much to take. Her picture of a passive woman who can gain control over her life only by becoming a victim is truly frightening. Less squeamish readers will extract a feminist message: in a society such as this, how else can a woman like Erika behave?' *New York Times Book Review*

'With formidable power, intelligence and skill she draws on the full arsenal of derision. Her dense writing is obsessive almost to the point of being unbearable. It hits you in the guts, yet is clinically precise' *Le Monde*

The Piano Teacher (2001) was directed by Michael Haneke, and starred Isabelle Huppert and Benoit Magimel. It won the Grand Prize of the Jury and Huppert and Magimel were awarded the Cannes Grand Prix as Best Actress and Best Actor in 2001. On DVD from all good retailers & online.

We Need to Talk About Kevin
Lionel Shriver

'This startling shocker strips bare motherhood . . . the most remarkable Orange prize victor so far' Polly Toynbee, *Guardian*

'Once in a while, a stunningly powerful novel comes along, knocks you sideways and takes your breath away: this is it . . . a horrifying, original, witty, brave and deliberately provocative investigation into all the casual assumptions we make about family life, and motherhood in particular' *Daily Mail*

'An awesomely smart, stylish and pitiless achievement. Franz Kafka wrote that a book should be the ice-pick that breaks open the frozen seas inside us, because the books that make us happy we could have written ourselves. With *We Need to Talk About Kevin*, Shriver has wielded Kafka's axe with devastating force' *Independent*

'One of the most striking works of fiction to be published this year. It is *Desperate Housewives* as written by Euripides . . . A powerful, gripping and original meditation on evil' *New Statesman*

The film of *We Need to Talk About Kevin* is in production, for release in 2011, directed by Lynne Ramsay, and starring Tilda Swinton and John C. Reilly.

Shoedog
George Pelecanos

'A model exercise in dysfunction and doomed American cool' *Guardian*

'The coolest writer in America' *GQ*

'The kind of book you are always hoping to find but rarely do' James Sallis

'Pelecanos has carved out a territory – the seedier suburbs of Washington, DC – and a language of danger and sadness all his own' *Chicago Tribune*

'A consummate stylist with a rare sense of contemporary slam-bang and angst' *Time Out*

'Washington DC's Zola' *Publishers Weekly*

'George Pelecanos has broken with tradition in so many ways, it feels as if he has launched a category of his own. Partly, it's his convincing evocation of an unfamiliar setting but mainly it's the feeling that we are definitely in the present – here is your first turn-of-the-century crime writer' Charlie Gillett

'Snaps with authentic street talk and with a switch-hitting plot . . . has something important to say about trust and treachery' *Washington Post*

The Book of Disquiet
Fernando Pessoa

'It could not have been written in England: there is too much thought racing hopelessly around. The elegance of the style, well conveyed in what seems to be a more than adequate translation, is an important component and a very ironic one. The diary disturbs from beginning to end . . . There is a distinguished mind at work beneath the totally acceptable dullness of clerking. The mind is that of Pessoa. We must be given the chance to learn more about him' Anthony Burgess, *Observer*

'Pessoa's near-novel is a complete masterpiece, the sort of book one makes friends with and cannot bear to be parted with. Boredom informs it, but not boringly. Pessoa loved the minutiae of what we care to deem the ordinary life, and that love enriches and deepens his art' Paul Bailey, *Independent*

'The very book to read when you wake at 3am and can't get back to sleep – mysteries, misgivings, fears and dreams and wonderment. Like nothing else' Philip Pullman

'It was a real bonus when Serpent's Tail published *The Book of Disquiet*, a meandering, melancholic series of reveries and meditations. Pessoa's amazing personality is as beguiling and mysterious as his unique poetic output. We cannot learn too much about him' William Boyd, *TLS Books of the Year*

'[A] classic of existential literature' Emma Tennant, *Independent on Sunday*

Devil in a Blue Dress
Walter Mosley

'A brilliant novel. Period. Mosley's prose is rich, yet taut, and has that special musical cadence that few writers achieve . . . I read *Devil in a Blue Dress* in one sitting and didn't want it to end. An astonishing first novel' Jonathan Kellerman

'A magnificent novel by Walter Mosley in which, from the first page, it's clear we have discovered a wonderful new talent . . . the most exciting arrival in the genre for years' *Face*

'A novel of astonishing virtuosity, upending Chandler's LA to show a dark side of a different kind' *Sunday Times*

'There is a splendid freshness to Mosley's prose and we sense that here is a real world we are hearing about for the first time' *Financial Times*

'For a writer who has the legacy of Chester Himes and more to live up to, Walter Mosley makes a distinctly confident start to his career' *Time Out*

Published in 1990, *The Devil in a Blue Dress* was awarded the John Creasey Award for the best first crime novel of the year.

Serpent's Tail

'Serpent's Tail is a consistently brave, exciting and almost deliriously diverse publisher. I salute you!' Will Self

'Nobody else has the same commitment to the young, the new, the untested and the unclassifiable' Jonathan Coe

'Serpent's Tail is one of the most unique and important voices in British publishing' Mark Billingham

'Serpent's Tail has made my life more interesting, enjoyable, exciting, easier' Niall Griffiths

'Serpent's Tail is a proper publisher – great writers, great books. If you want a favourite new author you've never heard of before, check their list' Toby Litt

'You're a good deed in a naughty world' Deborah Moggach

'Thanks, Serpent's Tail, for years of challenging reading' Hari Kunzru

www.serpentstail.com

Visit serpentstail.com today to browse and buy
our books, and to sign up for exclusive news and
previews of our books, interviews with our
authors and forthcoming events.

| NEWS | cut to the literary chase with all the latest news about our books and authors |

| EVENTS | advance information on forthcoming events, author readings, exhibitions and book festivals |

| EXTRACTS | read first chapters, short stories, bite-sized extracts |

| EXCLUSIVES | pre-publication offers, discounted books, competitions |

| BROWSE AND BUY | browse our full catalogue and shop securely |

FREE POSTAGE & PACKING ON ALL ORDERS...
WORLDWIDE

Follow us on Twitter • Find us on Facebook